THE
SLEEP
CLINIC

THE
SLEEP
CLINIC

A NOVEL

MICHELLE
YOUNG

Rock Forest Publishing

Cover Design by Michelle Young
Cover Photograph © Pixabay.com
Author Photograph © Youngs Photography

ISBN-13: 978-1-7750983-4-8

The Sleep Clinic / Michelle Young. – 1st ed.
Rock Forest Publishing

Printed by Imprimerie Gauvin
Gatineau, Québec

ALSO BY MICHELLE YOUNG

Salt & Light
Without Fear
Your Move
There She Lies

For John

"My mind is a home I'm trapped in
and it's lonely inside this mansion."
– Mansion, NF

CHAPTER 1

She visited me again last night. I'd sensed her presence before I'd even seen her. It happened the same way it always did. Yesterday was no different. No special reason for her to come around, no empty glass bottles for her to trip over, no jars of harmful pills to justify her social call.

I'd been minding my own business, attending to the growing pile of assignments I'd been neglecting all week after taking extra shifts at the drug store, when the hairs on the back of my neck began rising one by one, a tell-tale sign that I was being watched.

She always came to me when I had my back turned, always tried to catch me off guard. I'd been alone again in the small room, bent over my desk typing away, frantically trying to wrap my mind around the course material from Monday's lesson in Concepts in Sketching, Level 1. My notebook was covered in chicken scratch, my handwriting almost illegible. I'd been squinting to see the loops and curves of the letters when I felt her presence in my room.

She's been around a lot lately and I was naïve in thinking it was all the booze attracting her, like a beacon in the night guiding her to me. A direct line to my subconscious, a secret path to which only she had the map.

It is strange to admit, but I was getting used to finding her there, staring at my back with her wicked grin. As terrifying as she is, there's something about her—I can't put my finger on it.

I know I should be afraid, but her presence makes me feel a mixture of different emotions. None of it makes any sense to me, why I'm both excited and scared to death. If only I could figure out what's causing her to come visit then maybe it would all make sense. Why she comes around here every night, I have no idea, but I can't get her off my mind.

The soft tumble of racing feet makes the ground shake all around me as I sit on the cold floor. She's watching my every move. Her almond-shaped eyes stare right through me. The darkness in them almost sucks me in. The thin bridge of her nose perfectly fits her oval face, framed by shoulder-length wavy, dark hair. She's crouched strangely, un-human like. Her thin lips are stretched over sharp teeth, her canines on display. A disturbing snarl on her face shows an expression of content that makes my body shudder.

She scares me. I know that's the point.

I have to stop myself before I start picturing blood oozing out of her mouth.

"Dude, that's sick!" Tee exclaims, gazing over my shoulder.

A small smile plays on my lips as I bend over the paper to make a few adjustments to the piece in front of me. My hand cramps around the number 2B graphite pencil. I release the tool for a moment and make a fist, trying to ease the joint pain and get the blood flowing into my extremities.

"Thanks," I reply shyly, quickly grabbing hold of the pencil before it rolls off the page and lands on the hard floor, shattering the delicate interior and ruining the pencil forever.

I remember the time when I was a child and I'd dropped my favourite red pencil on the ceramic floor in the kitchen. The tip of it had popped right off and no amount of sharpening it would make it stick. The moment I would get the tip of the pencil sharp enough to my liking and put it against paper to draw in my colouring book, the tip would pop out once again. It was useless. One little clatter to the floor had broken my favourite color and there was no fixing it.

How desperately I'd clung to the tiny, needle tip-sized point between my thumb and forefingers, relentlessly trying to use what remained of the firetruck red tint, but I always ended up scraping my nails, bending them against the page pushing so hard to get the most of the broken piece, before giving up in frustration and throwing it in the trash along with the shavings. I had to wait until my birthday before my parents bought me a new colouring set so I could use my favourite red again. I'm much more careful with my pencils now. They are my prized possession. That and I worked hard to purchase them so I intend to make them last as long as deemed acceptable.

I don't want to stop drawing while the creative juices are flowing. Any distraction could make me lose her again. Staring at the page, I block out the bustling noises all around me and focus on the small details of the sketch. I make a few adjustments to the girl's cheekbones, highlighting them so that they appear more pronounced, then move on to her neckline, exaggerating the curves of her clavicles and the distinct dip between them.

She's alone in the drawing as she usually is when I think of her. I still haven't given her a name. I like the idea of her remaining nameless—mysterious—known only by a vague feeling. Mine alone. My mystery woman.

I shuffle myself closer to the wall and lean back against the community college lockers as Tee slides down beside me, peering intrigued at my latest piece.

"What are you going to call this one?" she asks as she takes an apple out of her backpack and sinks her teeth into it with gusto.

A splatter of apple juice lands on my denim jeans. I resist the urge to wipe it away immediately. Instead, I let the sweet bead of juice sit on the surface of my pants until it gets absorbed into the fibers of the fabric. It will dry and become unnoticeable within a few minutes, but I'll know I have a part of Tee with me for the rest of the day and that's a comforting thought.

I wonder what having this physical drawing in my possession does to me. It's the closest thing I can have to a photograph of this mystery woman. Constantly flipping between feeling comforted and paranoid, I want to believe that releasing her into the open and exposing her, even in drawing form, might release her hold on me somehow. That by drawing her out, making her real to others then maybe she will stop taking over my thoughts.

"I haven't decided yet," I say as I turn the drawing around in my hands, observing it from different angles to see if I've got all the dimensions right.

It's probably my most realistic portrait ever. I've managed to achieve the shading perfectly. Finally satisfied with the outline, I grab my pencil case in search of the next graphite pencils. Alternating between the 4B and 6B, I begin to darken the edges of her eyes, making them pop off of the page. The pencil does the work for me, I don't need to press hard to get the definition I want. Every strand of hair, every eyelash is explicitly drawn—very lifelike.

I'm somewhat hesitant to go over this one with my eraser. I typically like to clean up a sketch from all the initial composition, removing any obvious standard shapes used to draw people in accurate proportions, but something about this image makes me want to leave it messy and untamed. Almost like there's a layer of scratches or dust over the sketch, grain over film. In most sketches it would take away from the beauty I'm trying to capture in a portrait, but the imperfection seems to work in the sketch's favor this time. I will just have to trust my gut on this one.

I will leave the original sketch marks so that every layer of the drawing process can be seen if you know where to look for it. Nothing hidden. A mystery woman that has no secrets. It's very artistic of me to have even thought of this. The extra dimension and meaning makes it even better.

A sense of pride fills me as I move my clipboard towards Tee so she can examine the drawing more closely.

"Damn, Laurel. This chick is bad-ass!" she remarks, her eyebrows arched in surprise, clearly impressed.

I laugh and take the clipboard from her. "Thanks, I guess. Actually, I've been having a recurring nightmare of this chick," I say with a sideways glance to gauge her reaction. "She kind of scares the living crap out of me!" I say with a small laugh in case she doesn't take me seriously.

She knows me too well to make me feel embarrassed by my revelation. I don't need to worry about saving face with her. We stay seated in silence for a moment, both staring at the drawing between us, lost in thought.

A moment later, our eyes are still on the piece as she states, "You know what? She kind of looks like you." As though this fact was obvious and pointing it out to me was futile. My shocked expression makes her lips pucker.

"I mean, other than those fang-like teeth, all of her other features look just like you." She points out the piece and for the first time, I see exactly what she means. I almost drop the drawing right then onto the floor, letting a startling noise rattle through the halls but I don't. Instead, I cling to it even harder.

It's all I can do to keep the clipboard steady in my hand.

CHAPTER 2

My hands can't stop shaking as I walk to class, my backpack weighing heavily on my sore shoulders. I twist my neck to release the tension, but nothing changes; if anything, I've just made things worse.

The sketch I'd been so proud of only moments ago seems to weigh a thousand pounds in my bag. I should trash it. Get rid of it. Release the hold it has on me. But I know I won't. At least not yet.

I know myself. I will tear it out of my bag the instant I arrive home and stare at it for hours, analyzing every single detail, trying to figure out if what Tee said is true. That this mystery woman is, in fact, a self-portrait. I can't un-see it now that Tee has pointed it out. The realization gnaws at me.

I push through the classroom and find a seat in the second row, not too eager, but very aware of how distracted I can get when my mind wanders. I start to remove the items from my pack to get settled for class to begin when my fingers graze the portrait. I retract my hand as though I've been burned.

What is it about this woman? Her eyes aren't like mine. Mine are pale, hazel; hers are dark, sinister, and mean. I might be peculiar and the quiet type, but I've never been described as mean.

I stare at my hands and make fists with them—open them, stretch the fingers, and clench them again. There's no cracking of joints to justify the release of pain, just a silent, invisible ache. Doing this motion several times a day helps to ease the aching that throbs through my hands.

I shut my eyes and take a deep breath through my nose. I need to release my thoughts so that I can focus on class.

Mid-terms are coming up and I've been struggling with the material so far. I'm not hugely academic. I have trouble remembering specifics, like facts and dates. Sometimes the words seem to blur together, swirling like a gust of wind floating on the surface of the page, hovering, never quite reaching my brain. I've always struggled to retain this type of detailed information.

When I was younger, my parents arranged for me to complete a psychological assessment to determine if I had a learning disability.

Turns out I did, and a severe one at that.

My poor working memory is the major contributor to my struggles at school as it limits my ability to retain large amounts of information at one time before it gets stored into long-term memory. The tests had also revealed that I was dyslexic. I'd heard of this before as some of my other school friends struggled to read out loud when called on by the teacher, but not me. My dyslexia symptoms are different than those of my friends as mine have to do with trouble identifying numbers.

Thankfully, I've chosen a career path that works with my strengths rather than my weakness. I've picked this program specifically for the visual and creative aspects of it seeing as I've always excelled at those.

Talk of resident parties, bar crawls, and jell-o-shots bring me back to the room. I never get invited and I would probably decline if someone ever asked me to come to a party. It's funny, I used to love parties. I don't anymore. I'm quite content being the odd ball, the geek, the loner. Whatever it is they label it these days. I'm an introvert and I much prefer the company of my own thoughts, no matter how toxic they might get.

For most people, college is about finally enjoying opportunities they didn't have available back home; new experiences, trying things out, and making discoveries. For many of my friends, this was the highlight of going to study away from home. The freedom, no-rules, the access to drugs and alcohol, the making-up for lost time.

I don't care for any of that. I have too much work to catch up on and a daunting student loan to pay back. Every spare moment I have is either spent studying or working to pay what I owe.

The other students begin crowding the door as they enter and find their seats only moments before class begins. I wince at the sound of their sneakers squeaking as they drag their feet and mark up the glossy white tiles with black streaks. I hate that sound—like nails on a chalk board. Although the college got rid of the offensive lung-coating chalk years ago, I have no trouble remembering the sound from my childhood days. Like grinding teeth or a knife scratching a porcelain plate—cringe-worthy.

Thankfully, the entire college has opted for a modern education approach and has upgraded to new projectors and whiteboards in every classroom. I don't even feel sad at the thought that somewhere there's a steep mountain of horrible old chalkboards in a landfill.

The college has made great progress supplying us with the most up-to-date technology. Grateful that I don't have to use something ancient to learn on, I can't help but feel a sense of ownership in the new equipment I use every day. After all, I've paid for my share of it, I'm sure.

With the classroom door open, I spy the wall of live plants that fill the center of the building, balancing the starkness of the pure-white walls of the classroom by offering warmth and life. There are notes of light wood throughout the building and in the finish of the staple pieces. Minimalism seems to be taking off in the design world lately and the college appears to have adopted the look.

The smell of dry-erase markers fills my nostrils. I inhale deeply, trying to take in more of the fumes. I relax my shoulders and settle into the hard but curvy bamboo chair, gearing up for an hour-long lecture. If only the chairs came with armrests, then I could lean my heavy head in my hand, hold it upright with minimal effort, and pretend I'm not sleep-deprived. But alas, I must rely on my weak neck to do the job.

I play with my nose ring as my mind absentmindedly returns to the drawing in my backpack. What will I do with it when I get home? Should I show it to Xavier? What would he make of it? It's probably best not to show him. It would only worry him. My boyfriend reads a little too much into everything. I love him, but sometimes he can be a little dramatic and has a hard time letting things go.

I bite my lip. I hate censoring my days from him. I always feel guilty, like he knows I'm withholding something. He reads me like a book, knows all my expressions. He'll be able to tell, and then he'll get angry at me for not spilling it.

Bringing my hand to my mouth, I chew on a fingernail as I resolve to tell him only parts of the truth in order to pacify his curiosity and alleviate my guilt.

If the mystery woman shows up again, then I'll tell him everything. But for now, I'll keep her a secret.

CHAPTER 3

Walking home from the bus station takes me ten minutes. The outside lights are on when I reach my street. Class went on later than normal tonight as we cram for mid-terms. It's as though the syllabus was only there to appear organized when, in reality, we wasted the entire semester goofing off and now, weeks before the mid-terms, we are trying to learn everything we were meant to learn in three months.

I feel like I'm carrying an entire library in my backpack. My shoulders are sore, and I stick my thumbs under the straps to relieve them from the weight as I near the house. The sight of my front door is pure bliss. I long to reach it and remove my heavy backpack, sink into the softness of my mattress in peaceful silence before I have to drag my butt to my desk and study for several hours. I sigh. I'm not excited about it, but I know it must be done.

With my learning disability, I wasn't sure I'd get into any programs. I'd applied to so many, throwing spaghetti at the wall, hoping something would stick and that I'd get accepted somewhere, but I'd mostly received rejections. My grades weren't great. I only got into the program at Carter College because of my portfolio. My art saved me. The program director had called me on a Monday evening to personally congratulate me on my application and confirm my entry to the program.

I'd been so relieved to get in that I'd dropped the corded phone, almost smashing it onto my parent's kitchen floor. Thankfully, the cord had restrained the device inches short of the hard surface, keeping it dangling until I'd snapped out of the shock of the news and picked it back up. My parents had taken me out for ice cream to celebrate.

It had been a great day.

A small smile plays on my lips as I remember how proud I'd made my parents that day. The high of it had carried me through the rest of that summer, working overtime at the drugstore until I found a townhouse near campus while searching for a roommate.

I'd visited the house with my mom and dad and signed a one-year lease on the spot. They had been just as excited as I was, but behind my mother's smile, I could see heavy emotions of sadness playing in her eyes. She'd turned away and pretended to check cupboard space to avoid facing me and revealing how she really felt.

Leaving home hadn't been planned. In fact, it was a completely spontaneous decision. It was an opportunity to be closer to campus, minimizing my commute time by more than half, gaining independence, and forcing me to meet new people.

I unlock the door, grateful for the porch light one of my housemates left on for me. It's always nice to know someone else is home other than me.

Dropping my heavy bag in the entrance, I use my foot to shut the door behind me, remove my shoes, and shuffle towards the kitchen. My stomach is in knots and I'm starving. The clock on the wall states that it's half past nine. I moan internally. Another late night for me.

The kitchen is small and plain, but functional. With four people living here at any given time, it's easily the room that gets used the most—other than the single bathroom, of course. A house full of girls and only one bathroom isn't always easy to manage. There's a water-stained, handmade cleaning schedule, held on the fridge by a can opener magnet outlining the various rooms and responsibilities each housemate is in charge of on any given week.

Mondays are trash and recycling days, so that's the only one we keep alternating, but otherwise each of us is in charge of our own zones and tasks. I'm in charge of cleaning the bathroom weekly, but I haven't had time to do it yet this month. Someone must have gotten tired of waiting because I noticed the familiar bleach smell the other day. I make a mental note to pick up the slack whenever my mid-terms are through.

As there are so many of us living in the small house, the lead housemate, Nova, suggested that we each print our class and work schedules and plaster them on our bedroom doors to help us work around each other's schedules and avoid any issues. This works great, most of the time, except on the weekends when most of us have our boyfriends over. Then everything goes out the window and it's every woman for herself.

Another way Nova ensures smooth living conditions is by assigning individual cupboards to each housemate. I'm the proud owner of two large shelves in the pantry beside the fridge. I also have a designated shelf in the fridge and share part of a drawer with Rory, the housemate that lives in one of the basement rooms.

The house has three bedrooms on the top floor, which is where Nova's and mine are. I share a wall with the smallest bedroom that has been vacant ever since I moved in. Between Nova's and my room is the one and only bathroom with a leaky sink faucet. I can hear the single drops falling all night long—the walls are thin. I've gotten used to the steady tapping noise and wonder how I'll sleep once it's repaired—if it ever gets fixed, that is.

There are two more bedrooms in the basement, although those aren't exactly legal as you could barely fit a tissue box through the windows—not particularly useful in an emergency. Yet, the rent is cheap and the location is close to campus, so none of us complain. We have an unwritten rule of locking the front door even when one of us is home, and under no circumstance are we allowed to light candles.

I yawn as I stretch on my tippy toes to peer at my shelf in the kitchen. A downfall of being short is that it's a constant struggle to reach things without my stepstool. I think someone must have borrowed it recently as it's been misplaced and never returned. I consider climbing on top of the counter to reach my food better but resolve to back up until my back hits the opposite counter. Feeling victorious, I spot a box of macaroni and cheese and, without looking any further, reach for it using a wooden spoon, grunting as I stretch some more. The box falls down into my arms, and I search the bottom drawers for a pot.

As I move to the sink and begin filling the medium-sized pot, I text Xavier to let him know I've made it home safely, and that I'll give him a call later. He always worries about me when I'm out after dark.

With the phone in my hand, I begin to scroll through social media when I realize the pot is overflowing.

"Shit!" I mutter as I shut the tap off and pour out some excess water.

"I thought I heard you come in!" Ashley's chipper voice booms through the kitchen making me jump.

"Oh, hey!" I reply, splashing some water on my jeans, reminding me of Tee's apple splatter from earlier that's still embedded in the denim.

"I just got home not long before you, so I left the lights on," she adds, casually leaning against the counter in work-out clothes, her blond hair tied neatly in a high ponytail. Her pale, creamy skin is smooth, her eyes bright and makeup-free.

"Ah, thank you, I appreciate that." I place the pot on the burner and turn on the stove. Walking around her to get to the fridge, I mention, "It's starting to get darker earlier already. Can you believe it?" They're just words, no substance. I find Ashley a little intimidating. She just seems so put together, especially compared to me.

I just don't have it in me to make conversation tonight. My heart isn't in it. Thankfully, Ashley doesn't linger. Nodding at me, she grabs an orange and heads for the door, grabbing her gym bag on the way out.

How she still has energy after working a full shift at the hospital astonishes me. Ashley rents the other basement room, opposite Rory's. She got here a year before me and works odd hours—shift work. I could never do what she does. I'm messed up as it is with my somewhat normal schedule. I don't know how she does it.

Once my dinner is made, I bring the piping hot bowl up to my room to eat while I study today's material. I quickly realize I'm ravenous and devour the entire bowl in five minutes. Seeing my backpack on the floor leaning sadly against the wall, I debate reaching inside to inspect the mystery woman drawing more closely. Surprising myself, I manage to change my mind and focus on what really needs my attention.

I'm a few chapters behind on this week's readings, so I skim through it to see if there's any sections I need to revise more thoroughly. Thankfully, a lot of it makes sense so I take some notes, careful to write as neatly as possible as most of them turn illegible by the time the night's over.

I shake a few chocolate candies free from the cardboard box I keep on my desk as motivation for studying and pop a few in my mouth. I suck on them until all the colour melts away and I'm left with white shells of chocolate.

A few hours later, my phone pings next to me on my desk, breaking my train of thought. It's a message from Xavier.

Hey babe. Going to call soon?

I check the time on my laptop. It's already midnight. Time for bed. I rub my eyes, stand up from my desk chair, and change into my pajamas, a simple grey t-shirt and flannel pants. I make my way to the bathroom to do my nighttime wash-up and bump into Nova on the way.

"Hi Nova, how's it going?" I ask her tiredly, suppressing a yawn. "How's the studying coming along?" I add as I follow her into the bathroom. I yawn and cover my mouth.

The faucet drips away, the sound almost hypnotic, making me sleepy. It's not unusual for us to meet in here before bed. We have similar schedules and even work at the drug store together. It's actually how we met. We both got transferred to the store near campus as they needed people to work evenings and weekends. Being the desperate students we are, we both jumped at the opportunity. She'd told me about the house she was living in, mentioned a room becoming available, and offered to give me a tour.

"Ugh, you know...I'm over my head in textbooks." She sighs as she brushes her teeth with rigor and spits into the sink.

I think I see some blood in her spit mixed with the goopy blue toothpaste and feel a twinge of pity for her. I might be messy and not have my life together, but Nova tries to control every single aspect of hers. It must drive her crazy. I know Nova struggles with anxiety and always wants everything done just so, but I worry about her. She doesn't know how to relax, to let her hair down. Observing her now, I see the sunken cheeks, the dark circles under her eyes. Stress affects us all in different ways. I tend to eat excessively, but Nova forgets to eat anything at all.

I watch as Nova wipes her mouth with the back of her hand and grabs a washcloth to wash her face. She doesn't wear any make-up, unlike Ashley. Her eyes are big and a bright blue that seems to sparkle without any help from eye shadow. She's been blessed with thick eyelashes and beautiful porcelain-like skin—smooth and perfect. She has thin and naturally rose-tinted lips. Her only flaw is her crooked teeth. In a way, I find this small imperfection makes her even more beautiful.

"Any news on finding a tenant for the spare room?" I enquire.

The extra housemate would help reduce our shares of the utility bills. As Nova is the lead housemate and found each of us, we're all hoping she'll fill the spot soon. The landlords also give her a bonus payout if she finds someone without them needing to place an ad online. It saves them the hassle as Nova does the search, performs the interviews, and offers the tour of the house. Our landlords live a few hours away, so repairs are typically done on a monthly basis rather than right away. However, they haven't come by once since I've lived here, hence the leaky sink faucet in the bathroom.

"Nothing yet. Maybe I should have just signed on that other chick I met at the coffee shop during the summer," she ponders out loud.

"Wasn't she like a hardcore partier?" I remind her.

"Yeah, but the money would have been nice. These textbooks are costing me a fortune!" She rubs her forehead, tension building.

And with that, Nova waves goodnight and pads over to her bedroom, shutting and locking her door behind her. I finish up and do the same.

Pulling the comforter over my body, relishing the fluffy down enveloping me, I feel like I'm on a cloud. My muscles protest against the soft bed, the shock of something so soft after sitting in my office chair for the last few hours. My thighs have grown numb from lack of circulation, so I rub my hand over the tight muscles to get the blood flowing.

Laying my head on the pillow, I start counting sheep. It might be juvenile, but it works for me. Within minutes I'm fast asleep and dead to the world.

CHAPTER 4

I hear a loud banging at my door and find myself standing on top of my bed, right in the center of the mattress. I'm still wearing pajamas and my hair is wet and sticking to my face.

"What the hell?" I say as I sit down and slide off the bed, alarmed.

"Laurel? Are you okay in there?" The banging continues.

Recognizing her voice, I rush to the door to unlock it and open it up to a frazzled, sleep-deprived Nova.

"What's going on? Are you okay?" I ask, scanning her body, trying to understand the reason for her urgent banging.

"I just asked you that!" she screams but then takes a deep breath, controlling herself. "Sorry," she adds. "You just scared the crap out of me! What the hell were you doing in there? I thought someone was attacking you!" She gestures inside my bedroom and we both turn to notice the state of the room.

Confused, I take in the sheets twisted tight like a rope and the comforter lying on the parquet flooring in a pile. One pillow has been shredded and the other one is at the foot of the bed. The drapes have been ripped from their curtain rings and are hanging on for dear life. There are objects thrown haphazardly around the room. It's a total disaster.

"Wow." Nova breathes out, her eyes as big as saucers as she takes it in. "What in the world...?" Too shocked by the state of the room, she doesn't finish her thought.

I can't blame her. I'm at a loss for words as well. Bewildered, we both stare at the mess for a few moments before she seems to shake it off and snaps her attention back to me.

"Are you okay, Laurel?" Her eyebrows inch closer together in concern as her gaze travels all over my face and my body, much like I've just inspected her for any signs of why she'd be pounding on my door in the middle of the night.

My mind races as I try to make sense of why my room is in such a chaotic state, but I can't find any reason for it.

"I honestly don't know what happened," I offer pathetically.

I chew on the inside of my cheek, searching my mind for an explanation. This is crazy! Did I do this to my room? How come I don't remember any of it?

"All I heard was you screaming your head off and then crashing noises. It was terrifying! I thought someone had broken in. I thought you were getting killed or something!" She half-heartedly laughs, seeing as I'm alive and well, but the relief is short lived as her eyes quickly well up with tears, as the fear begins to take over.

Seeing her crying breaks my heart. I feel awful. I rush over to her and wrap her in a hug, only to realize how sweaty I am. I back off and stand awkwardly in front of her as she wipes her eyes. I hadn't understood that my hair was wet from sweat and not from a late shower which I sometimes take before bed.

"Sorry," I muster finally. *What's going on?* I wonder to myself. "I'm so sorry, Nova. I have no clue what happened."

I scan the room once more and find my phone resting on my nightstand. I step inside, and in two strides, I've reached the little table. I pick up my phone and check the time—two in the morning. I've only been asleep for two hours, then.

"Look, I'm fine. I'm not sure what happened. It was probably just a nightmare or something," I say, trying to be reassuring as I flip the phone over in my hand—a nervous habit of mine.

Remembering the chocolate candies, I explain, "I ate some chocolate while I was studying. Must have caused some strange dreams." I attempt to laugh it off.

"That was more than a reaction to chocolate, Laurel." Nova's voice and stare are deadpan. She doesn't believe any of it. "Do you remember what the dream was about?" she asks finally.

"No idea. I don't remember dreaming at all." I shrug apologetically. "But it's okay. I'll be fine." I smile at her, trying to sound reassuring.

She bites her lip, unsure. I haven't convinced her, which is no surprise because I'm having a hard time convincing myself. Yet, the longer we stand here trying to make sense of what's happened, the quicker morning will come.

"Listen, let's go back to bed for now, we both have to get up really early." I rub at my neck, the tension annoyingly still present. "I'll stop by the store on the way home from work tomorrow to grab a new pillow. It'll be okay." I'm trying to fix what I can control, but my thoughts are distant.

Why can't I remember what happened? And why was I standing in the middle of my bed?

"Okay, if you're sure. Maybe leave your bedroom door unlocked for the rest of the night, just in case you need help," Nova suggests as she rubs hard at her eyes.

When she opens them again, there are angry red veins in the whites of them, making them appear glassy and dirty. For the second time tonight, we say goodnight and return to our respective rooms. Somehow, my screaming didn't seem to have woken up anyone else. I sigh, feeling grateful for that tiny mercy.

Still clutching my phone in my hand, I notice a missed call from Xavier.

"Shit!" I completely forgot to call him after I finished studying. The bed had been so comfortable that I'd simply fallen asleep. I hurriedly text him to let him know I'm sorry for missing his call and that I'll call him in the morning.

Rubbing my forehead, I begin to clean up the mess I've made, focusing mainly on the essentials. I'm too tired to deal with the clutter right now; it will have to wait. Lying in bed, I feel a sharp pain on my arm. Turning on the light I notice a deep gash on my forearm that wasn't there before. Droplets of blood have stained my white sheets and I swear under my breath. I grab a nearby tissue and wrap it around my arm to cover the wound, too lazy to get up and grab a bandage from the bathroom.

This will have to do for now.

I breathe in deeply and try to sleep, but for the rest of the night I toss and turn, worried that something is wrong with me.

I hadn't wanted to admit to Nova that I could remember slivers of what happened. Not images, but rather the emotions I felt. I remember feeling utterly terrified and running from something. Or rather someone. Someone that strongly resembled the mystery woman from my drawing.

CHAPTER 5

By five in the morning, I give up on sleep altogether and get up. I have a big day ahead of me, and even more to do now as I need to clean up this mess. As I begin to tidy up, my phone buzzes. Xavier is calling me.

"Hey, babe, sorry I forgot to call last night," I begin, but he interrupts me.

"Do you know how worried I was?" His tone is indignant, and I freeze at the harshness of it. *What's his problem?*

"Babe, I texted you when I got in, but then I lost track of time and fell asleep. You can't possibly be mad at me for that." I sound defensive even to myself. It's not how I mean to sound. I shouldn't feel guilty. I haven't done anything wrong. I was doing long hours these days and I was exhausted. "Look, I'm really sorry I forgot to call and that you were worried," I finally say to appease him.

Pressing the phone to my ear, I realize I'm holding my breath standing still in the middle of my bedroom waiting for a reply from him, but I only get the silent treatment. My apology isn't going to cut it this time. It's not the first time I've slipped up like this. I always forget to call him. I should probably feel a little bit bad, but I don't.

I feel like Xavier forgets how life is for me these days. While he lives at home and his parents make his meals, I have to do everything on my own. The groceries, the laundry, the meal planning, the cleaning—all of this plus going to college and working every spare moment takes a lot out of me. Sometimes things slip my mind.

I hold my ground and remain quiet as well, not wanting to apologize again when it didn't even feel right the first time.

"Alright," I hear him say finally. "So, are you still planning on coming up this weekend?" he asks, annoyance in his tone.

"Yeah, I'm thinking of packing up my stuff tonight so that I can get to your place right after class tomorrow. I'll just take the bus straight from campus and head over." The bus ride was pretty straight-forward, with one transfer in the middle. It was a long ride, but it would allow me to catch up on my readings.

"Okay, cool!" he says, sounding suddenly chipper. "My parents are going to a wedding Friday night, so we'll have the place to ourselves." And now I understand why he's so excited.

We haven't been alone in a while. Every time I've come home to visit him, his parents have also been there, hovering around like vultures. There's zero privacy when they're around. He hasn't said anything, but I know he's expecting to get laid. The prospect of sex is the furthest thing from my mind right now, but I feel like I should make an effort. It's been several weeks since we've been intimate, as I've chosen to stay here and focus on work and my studies.

As we discuss specifics, I pick up some random items around me and catch my reflection in the mirror hanging from my bedroom door. I look ragged. My hair is a frizzy halo of curls from sweating last night and there are deep purple crescents under my eyes. When I go to touch my face, I see the cut on my forearm. I'd forgotten about it, distracted by the mess in the room.

As Xavier talks about a new song he's been working on, strumming a few strings on his classical guitar as a preview of the melody, I pull the sheets off the bed to reveal a ghastly looking bedsheet. My tissue hadn't done a proper job stopping the blood as there were rusty streaks and splatters staining the white fabric.

How could so much blood come from one cut? I inspect it again now to confirm that I don't need stitches. From my quick assessment, I will be just fine. The skin has a blueish tint to it around the cut, followed by a larger yellow bruise around it, but the cut itself appears to be drying up. It will scab over and, in a few weeks, it will be gone. I may have a slight scar, but it will go practically unnoticed. I make a mental note to purchase new sheets as well as a new pillow when I go to the store.

I stare at the mess surrounding me, amazed, and realize Xavier asked me a question.

"Sorry, what was that?" I refocus on our conversation and tell him I need to get a shower in before heading to work.

We hang up and I race around the room picking up loose feathers from my pillow. Thankfully the ceiling fan wasn't running, or it would have looked like a tornado of dead birds in here.

Satisfied with my quick clean-up job for the moment, I get in the shower and focus on rinsing most of the blood from the cut as best as I can before heading to work.

Time seems to drag on forever. Thursdays are typically busy shifts for me, but with mid-terms coming up, the College Square drug store is unusually quiet.

My manager has already sent two other cashiers home early and I might go next if things don't pick up soon. As much as I want to go home and rest or study, I need the money, so I busy myself making sure there are enough plastic bags at each cash for when the rush does come. I count my till and unroll more coins to pass the time. My legs hurt from standing still and having nothing to do.

I wander through the aisles and help stock the shelves. Happy to feel useful, I get lost in the repetitive task. The music blares through the speakers; someone must have turned it up as no customers have come in for several hours.

Even though it's a warm day, I opted to wear my long-sleeved uniform shirt today. I didn't want to answer any questions about the cut on my arm. I wouldn't even know what to say if anyone asked. Best to hide it for now.

There are so many questions swirling around in my mind that I'm struggling to focus. When a customer finally does come into the store, I give them the wrong change and hit my hip on the open cash register which I should have remembered to shut.

It's a company policy to always close your register when you step away from the cash or when handing out change. It helps ensure the money remains in the till. Feeling clumsy and tired, I feel myself getting hot from embarrassment.

In the last hour of my shift, I'm stocking shelves when I open a supplier's box filled with packages of Melatonin pills which are supposed to help with sleep. I linger over the box a moment and take a jar of the capsules in my hand. Turning it around, I read the label and decide to try them out. I buy a smaller quantity and, when my shift finally ends, head over to the store to replace the items I've destroyed during the night.

I'm feeling hopeful having found the pills and in control since I'm taking steps to return everything to normal. It will be like it never happened and I'll be able to put this whole thing behind me.

CHAPTER 6

Nearing home, I notice the outdoor lights aren't on today which means I'm the first to arrive for the night. As the fall weather approaches, so do the increasingly strong winds that rip through the night and the imminent threat of rain. I hurry as best I can, holding on to the shopping bag containing my new pillow and sheets.

I wanted to change after work before heading to the store which is why I'd brought along my backpack. I thought the sheets might fit inside it and I'd have less to carry in my arms, but the zipper on my bag wouldn't close and, in the end, I opted to carry everything.

I want nothing more than to run to reach our front door as quickly as possible. It takes everything for me to keep a steady pace. The sky grows darker as I step onto the porch. Its inky blackness expands towards the horizon, revealing a few bright stars, reminding me just how small I truly am. Large grey clouds roll in the distance, at once covering clusters of stars and parts of the full moon hanging in the sky. Tonight would be perfect for a traditional Halloween night, but as it turns out, I hate creepy things. I feel childish for being afraid of the dark.

Our house is the last one in a row of attached townhomes. There's a walking trail along the side of the house, but I tend to avoid using it. Even in the daytime, the empty trail frightens me.

Rain begins to fall in sheets soaking my back. I twist myself awkwardly to fish my keys from the front pocket of my backpack and notice a girl walking through the parking lot to her house. She marches confidently in the dark, stepping through rain puddles as though she's unaffected by her surroundings. Not that I fear getting wet, but she seems to taunt the rain, walking through it as though she owns it, her body language seeming to say, *Try me.* Her confidence seeps out of her, elevated by her steady walk. A part of me shrinks as I watch her. I'm a mess in comparison. A weak little girl, clumsy and cumbersome.

My hand finally locates the key as I face the door, forcing the girl and her bravado out of my mind. As I turn the key in the lock, the wind picks up, rustling the bushes and leaves on the trail next to where I stand.

The noise startles me and inadvertently makes me drop my shopping bag. I grunt, feeling foolish and frustrated. As I scramble to pick it up, the bag rips against the rough surface of the front step. I grab the items individually, but the wet ground has made the plastic coating on the sheets slippery. My fingers feel cold and refuse to grip the packages. I tuck them under my arm and feel a sense of urgency to get inside and nail the door shut behind me.

Turning the deadbolt will have to do for now.

Still, I can't shake the feeling of not being truly alone. Terrified that something is lurking in the darkness, I turn on all the lights.

The floor is marked with mud tracks and puddles from where I stepped haphazardly with my soiled running shoes, but somehow, I'm already beginning to feel safer. I don't mind this kind of mess. This is easy to clean—it gives me purpose. A task to occupy my mind and pull it away from the thoughts that paralyze me.

Dropping my newly purchased items in a semi-dry zone of the floor, I remove my soiled shoes and walk to the kitchen for some paper towels to wipe down the floor until all evidence of my pathetic fear is erased. Placing my shoes on the mat by the door, I grab my items and race up the stairs, taking two steps at a time.

I didn't lock my room when I left this morning, so there's no delay when I arrive at the top of the landing and swing the door open. The sight is astonishing. It hadn't looked this offensive this morning after my quick tidying up, but then again, I'd been distracted by Xavier's call. I sigh, looking around at the magnitude of the disarray around me. More things to tidy up. I want to clean this mess as quickly as possible so that I can resume studying, as I know I won't be doing many assignments this weekend with Xavier around.

I'm excited to see him. I miss his warm hugs and his reassuring soft snores at night. I remember that I need to pack my overnight bag tonight to bring it with me tomorrow, so I begin placing my extra pajamas in the bag along with my toothbrush, hairbrush, and birth control pills.

Digging inside my backpack, I retrieve the sleeping pills I purchased at work, turn the cap, and break the seal.

"Worth a try," I mumble as a yawn threatens to come out. *I hope these work*, I think to myself as I pop a tablet in my mouth, washing it down with stale water sitting in a mug on my dresser.

The capsule's plastic coating sticks to my throat as it reluctantly slides its way down until it gets lodged in the middle, not quite reaching my stomach. The sensation makes me gag, so I swallow more water. When I'm certain the pill has dislodged and is now dissolving in my stomach acid, I continue packing my bag.

My fingers land on the clipboard with the drawing of the mystery woman. I pull it out carefully with shaking fingers. I force myself to stare at it and try to conjure memories of last night's dream but come up empty. Whatever caused me to jump on the bed last night wasn't like any nightmare I've ever had. There had been no distinct images, only strong emotions.

Before I realize what I'm doing, I grab a blank page from the printer tray, on the top of my dresser and pull out my graphite pencils from my backpack. I start outlining a figure with a faint line and then add darker shadows, enhancing various parts of the image until it becomes recognizable. It's different from the first one, but here in front of me, I've got an image of the same woman that's been haunting me. Those eyes, empty and black, stare right through the page and through my soul.

I shiver.

In response, I feel my stomach rumbling. Glancing at my phone, I noticed that several hours have trickled by without me noticing. I've completely missed dinner. This often happens when I get lost in a drawing.

I decide to grab a banana from my cupboard and a slice of bread that I plan to coat in smooth peanut butter. It will be good enough for tonight. However, when I open my cupboard, I have a hard time locating my bananas. I pull out the peanut butter jar and the box of granola to peek behind them but find none.

Where are they? I just bought them the other day. I couldn't be out already. Confused and annoyed, I resort to eating only a slice of bread, spreading on the peanut butter aggressively, almost ripping the soft bread. Downing some milk along with it, I feel somewhat satisfied with my meal and head back up the stairs.

Shutting my bedroom door behind me, I hear the wind howling against the sides of the house making the siding creak with every gust. I grab the throw from the edge of my bed and wrap it around my shoulders as I slip my bare feet into the plush slippers Xavier got me for Christmas last year. I'm shivering and contemplate taking a quick shower to warm up, but instead I stubbornly flip through my notes and try my best to distract my mind, fooling it into believing I'm warmer than I feel.

It takes several minutes before the chill finally begins to leave my body, and I feel comfortable. Sitting at my desk, scratching my head, my eyelids begin to feel heavier.

The pill must be working its magic. I smile, feeling triumphant. *Right on time.* Relieved and excited at the prospect of getting some sleep tonight, I eagerly begin my nighttime routine.

I don't bump into Nova tonight while getting into the bathroom. She must still be up studying, but when I peek at her door, I only spot darkness coming through the crack at the bottom. *Maybe she went to bed early? I did wake her up horribly this morning.*

Feeling sluggish, I crawl into bed, my limbs heavy. I'm on the verge of dozing off when I hear a loud noise, a sort of scraping sound that makes my skin crawl.

It sounds like someone is pulling a heavy piece of furniture across the floor. It's a terrible sound and completely out of place this late at night. I sit upright in bed and feel myself growing tense as my ears strain to hear the noise better.

It seems to be coming from the room on the other side of my wall, only that room's empty. Isn't it?

Maybe Nova had rented it after all, although that would be extremely quick, as she'd only just mentioned something about it last night. Yet I do recall discussing with Nova that the girl might not be a good fit. So, if not a new housemate, then who would be moving furniture around at this time of night?

Feeling somewhat irritated but also curious, I hesitantly open my bedroom door and peek into the dark hallway. It's pitch black, save for the blue hue of my cell phone illuminating my steps. I walk over to the room next to mine and knock softly on the door, worried about disturbing whoever's inside and not wanting to cause another scene to wake up Nova.

Wrapping my arms around myself to keep warm, the sudden jarring noise having pulled me away from my warm new sheets, I hop from one leg to the other. While I wait for an answer, I hold my breath and stand very still, trying to make out any sounds which might explain whose presence is beyond the door. Trying my ear against the door yields no answers. No one comes to open it, and there's only silence on the other side. Either there's no one there, or someone is doing their best to keep quiet in the hope I will give up and leave them to it.

"What the hell?" I say under my breath. I shake my head and head back to my room, closing the door with a tight click. I hesitate a moment, debating with myself, but after quick deliberation, I leave the door unlocked as per Nova's suggestion.

Lying in bed, I come up with explanations for the noise. Perhaps someone was in the kitchen having a late-night snack as I'd done. I could easily verify this but having finally settled back under the warm sheets makes the prospect of getting out of bed again more than daunting. The other option is that someone in the house attached to ours is moving furniture late at night. Even though this is plausible, it seems extremely unlikely.

Before I can think of a reasonable explanation with which I'm satisfied, the pills take over and I quickly drift off to sleep.

CHAPTER 7

I awake feeling lethargic. I didn't wake once through the night and had no dreams—good nor bad. Yet, I can't say whether I feel rested or not. It's as though the sleeping pills knocked me out but didn't let me rest or recharge.

I push myself to my feet and spot my overnight bag in the corner of the room, a reminder that I'm spending the weekend with Xavier. A jolt of excitement courses through me at the thought of seeing him. He wants to play me more of the song he's been working on.

Xavier has been playing guitar since he was seven and he's extremely talented. He's got a unique take on country and reggae music that people love. He's been playing for large crowds at local fairs and high school proms, but he wants more. It's his hope that he can make this his career one day. He has dreams of recording his own music someday and of touring around the world, playing his music for others to enjoy. He works at a restaurant as a bartender to save up enough money to get into a recording studio next year.

He's always a hit, especially with teenage girls. He's got that bad boy look, a messy hairdo that falls over his baby blue eyes, and a raw voice that's out of this world. Just thinking about him makes me weak in the knees. I hadn't realized how much my body craves his touch.

I'm also looking forward to the day as our class is supposed to be learning the business of design as well as the mastery of colour and topography in graphic design. I've been excited to take this course for a while, since professionals in the field will be sharing their knowledge with us.

On my desk are the side-by-side sketches I've made of the same woman. Hesitating, I glance at them, my lip curling. *What has been happening to me? Why do I keep seeing this woman?*

I decide to leave them behind for the time being. I'll talk to Xavier about it soon, but I'm not ready quite yet. We've been together since high school, but if I'm going crazy, I'd like to find out before he does.

Some distance from my sketches might do me some good. After all, I didn't conjure the woman in any dreams last night. Perhaps the sleeping pill was the answer after all. I'll have to take it again tonight to see how it affects me.

Getting ready to hop in the shower, I walk down the hall and peer at the door next to mine for any hints as to what I'd heard last night, but the door remains stubbornly shut. It must have been my imagination.

Reaching for the door handle of the bathroom, I realize that it's locked before I notice the sound of the shower running. Nova must be having a shower. It's not her usual shower time, but maybe she's running late this morning. I head back to my room and sit at my desk to wait her out.

Minutes pass by, and forty-five minutes later, the shower is still running with no sign of slowing down. Glancing at my phone I realize I'm going to be late if Nova doesn't get out soon. Debating what to do, I chew on a cuticle until it rips off between my teeth. Finding my courage, I go knock on the door and call her name, but she doesn't answer. I knock louder, but still nothing.

I begin to worry. What if Nora fell and hit her head while showering? What if she's unconscious?

I deliberate what the right thing to do is, but quickly decide that I need to break down the door. Using my shoulder, I slam against it as hard as I can, sending pain radiating through my jaw and head. I wiggle the doorknob and try again. This time, the door swings open.

The room is empty. Only steam and a very hot running shower. Concern switches to confusion. Why would someone turn on the shower, lock the door, and leave? It makes no sense. Between the missing food, the sound of furniture scraping on the floor, and the empty shower, I feel like my housemates have been replaced by ghosts. Maybe I am losing my mind after all.

My phone chirps, reminding me that I'm pressed for time. Pushing aside worry and the mixture of feelings I'm experiencing, I hop into the shower to wash quickly, hoping there's still hot water left and that the soap will wash away all the strangeness from the last twenty-four hours.

Class is quiet today. Everyone is feeling the pressure of mid-terms coming up. Those that usually joke around or come in late are there before me. I follow close behind them but am forced into selecting a chair at the back of the classroom. The other students must be eager for the front seats today.

I bite my lip absentmindedly as I slump down in my seat. I can feel a slight headache coming on. I'm exhausted, and my brain feels fried. My hands are shaky and my heart thumps at an alarming rate. The room spins around me as I realize that in my rush this morning, I've missed my breakfast. Reaching a hand in my bag, I'm grateful to discover a squished granola bar. Unwrapping the treasure, I eagerly bite into the sweet oats and chocolate chips. I'm starving.

At the sound of my chewing, some students lift their heads as though I'm being incredibly rude. I get a few stares before they turn their noses back to their manuals. Other than my apparently loud chewing, the only other sounds in class are the sharp turning of pages, the teacher's typing, and the tick-tock of the ancient clock above the classroom door.

The teacher is quieter than normal as well. She's typing away on her computer, ignoring us until the final possible minute, when class begins. She looks agitated by something on her computer. Her brows are furrowed together, her lips pursed tight. She pouts like she's attempting a fish-lip selfie. Her fingers fly over the keyboard, making a loud tapping sound. Her eyes never leave the screen, she's completely enthralled by what she's doing.

I glance anxiously at the clock. The tick-tock noise coming from the minute and hour hands seems to echo in the room. I hear a fly overhead hitting the ceiling light repeatedly. Pages turn furiously as the teacher types, punctuating every letter as though it's the keyboard she's irritated with and not the person she's writing to. She hasn't made any movements to indicate that class has begun. No one else seems to notice. No one but me, that is.

I remove a metallic ruler from my pencil case and let it clatters loudly on the ground, attempting to break the trance everyone seems to be in. It works.

The teacher peers up from her computer, releases her mouth from its fish-shaped prison, and glances at the clock. Her eyes grow large in alarm as she realizes she's late to get the lesson started.

Cracking her hands quickly, she begins to gather papers and stands up, taking a sip of her coffee. It must have grown cold because her face contorts as she scowls at it, taking offence at the drink. If she hadn't been in front of an entire classroom full of students, she probably would have spit it right back into her mug, but instead I watch her recoil as she forces herself to swallow the bitter cold liquid. I feel for her. She's usually not this distracted.

I guess she and I have that in common these days.

I allow my mind to speculate, pondering what might have stolen her away from her duties. A lover's spat perhaps. An online order delayed once again. Or maybe she was writing a letter to the administration, explaining the shortage of white board markers that keep disappearing from classrooms.

I watch her intently as she shuts off her computer, walks around the desk to lean on it and faces the class. She gives nothing away. I guess I'll never know why she was so bothered and taking out her anger on her computer.

She drops her stack of papers on the surface of the desk and claps her hands together to announce the beginning of class. Finally. I snap out of it, shake off the imaginary life of my teacher and return my attention to my own.

One by one, I watch the students shut their books and glance up, red-eyed from late night study sessions, yet expectant and ready for instruction. People respect her. I admire that. I wish I had that kind of power. Instead, I've settled for blending in. I'm a wallflower, not wanting to be seen, but watchful. I don't need the attention or the added responsibility of anyone looking to me as a role model or as a guide to being the perfect student. My life is quiet, predictable, and safe. I'm nothing special and I'm happy to leave it that way. I'm just trying to survive college and get my certificate.

I have big dreams of working at a marketing agency when I'm done, designing posters and creating ads for large corporations. I'm not as advanced as some of the other students in my program and have a long learning curve ahead of me with regards to the computer programs we're being taught, but what I have cannot be taught.

It's pure—instinctive. I simply have an eye for this stuff. Always have. It's difficult to explain, but I find it easy to do things that others might spend hours learning from books or YouTube videos. It's just ingrained in me, as though I was born with this knowledge or skill right from the get-go.

Many of my teachers have mentioned this to me, astonished when I admit that I've received no formal training, that I've always been able to do it. I just need more confidence to let that side of me shine so the rest of the world sees it.

Lately, I've been working on a special project. I've been reluctant to share it with anyone while it's still at the beginning stages. The only person I've shown it to is Xavier. I'm too nervous to show anyone else. It's a contemporary design using a mix of old washed-out photographs and colourful maps blended together. It's supposed to represent where we've been and where we're going as a civilization. I'm quite proud of how it's turned out.

Xavier was absolutely ecstatic when I showed it to him on video call. He's always believed in me, which is why going away to college was easier. He practically pushed me out the door. I appreciate his support—I do—but sometimes I wonder if maybe he was trying to get rid of me.

CHAPTER 8

The bus ride to Xavier's is relatively uneventful. There aren't that many people heading to Cornwall on a Friday night, I guess. There's not much of anything out here. But for me, this is home.

It's where I'm from and where my family is. It's also where my boyfriend is waiting for me, sitting in his jet-black Honda as the bus pulls into the mall parking lot. Last stop. The three of us remaining passengers step off.

If I weren't carrying half my own weight in textbooks, I'd have skipped over to him. He looked incredibly handsome as he stepped out of the vehicle and leaned against it, crossing his arms over his toned pecs. He's wearing the black hoodie I got him for Christmas last year and has a new black Under Armour ball cap on backwards. He's so damn sexy. I lick my lips in anticipation.

We have the place to ourselves tonight. Suddenly, I feel foolish for having brought all this reading material with me. What in the world was I thinking? How will I possibly get any studying done this weekend?

I realize I'm rushing and catch myself. Tucking a stray strand of hair behind my ear to keep it from floating wildly in the wind, I force myself to slow my stride. I don't want to appear too eager. I don't know why I still feel the need to play this game. We've been a couple for over two years.

"Hey, sexy lady," he chants followed by a whistle, eyeing me up and down.

I have no idea what he finds attractive in me. I'm not much to look at, and I'm an entire foot shorter than he is. When I wrap my arms around him, my head lands on my favourite spot on his chest. He kisses the top of my head and I breathe out, finally letting go of the stress from the week.

"I've missed you," I whisper into his hoodie, inhaling the manly smells I've been yearning for weeks now.

I smile at him all doe-eyed, and he leans in, cupping my chin in his hand, lifting it slightly before pressing his lips to mine in a deep, passionate kiss that makes my knees buckle.

"Woah, down, girl," he laughs. "There'll be plenty of time for that later." He winks and grabs the backpack off my back, opens the back door of the car, and tosses it carefully in the backseat before getting in the driver's seat.

Sitting down next to him, I've barely got my seatbelt on when he grabs my face again for another kiss. We're like two starving wolves, hungry for each other's bodies. If his intensions weren't clear before, they are crystal clear now. I can't say I mind. I'm feeling it too.

We drive along and make small talk about people in town, Xavier's week, and when we should stop by to say hello to my family. Placing his hand behind the headrest as I adjust the radio dials, Xavier tells me he's got a special dinner planned for us—spaghetti and meatballs with garlic bread and a side of Caesar salad. He even made his own pasta sauce. Seriously sometimes I wonder if this guy is even real.

Acoustic guitar music plays softly from the computer speakers as we sit down for our romantic, candlelit dinner. Xavier pours me a generous glass of pinot noir and winks again. Charming me with atmosphere, food, and wine, he's pulling out all the moves tonight. I suddenly feel underdressed in my light sweater and jeans. Gingerly twirling the noodles around my fork, I'm surprised I don't splatter sauce all over myself. I feel nervous for some reason. Like I need to impress Xavier. Like I owe him something for making this elaborate meal. I know I'm just being silly, that I'm not used to getting spoiled, but my paranoid mind makes it difficult to enjoy myself fully.

Deciding to make the most of our time together, I do my best to stifle any doubts about his feelings for me that I've imagined. Here's a man who loves me, no matter what, and has made me a beautiful meal. The smells of fresh oregano, basil, and parmesan fill my nostrils as I take a healthy bite of the al-dente pasta. It's simply perfection—absolutely scrumptious.

"Babe, this is delicious!" I exclaim, feeling like I've been starving myself for the last few weeks. I haven't eaten anything with this much flavour in a long while. I let out an audible moan in appreciation as I shovel more food in my mouth, using a fork and spoon to swirl the noodles up to my mouth.

"That good, huh?" A smirk on his lips, Xavier eyes me over the flame of the tall candles. He's proud of himself, as he should be. He's an excellent cook and he's cute when he gloats.

"Hey, what's that?" He points to the scratch on my arm.

I'd almost forgotten about it. It had already started to heal, but purple and yellow bruising and a faint scar remained.

"Oh, that? It's nothing. I don't even know how it happened. I must have hurt myself while stacking shelves at work or something," I say, not sounding that convincing even to myself.

"Well, if it happened at work, you should definitely tell your manager about it. You could get worker's compensation for it. That looks like a pretty nasty cut." He's stopped eating altogether.

His concern for me is genuine and it makes me blush. Seeing how much he cares for me is what I love the most about him.

"I promise you, I'm totally fine." I smile up at him. Satisfied, he nods, and we resume devouring our meal in silence like a pack of hungry hyenas.

After dinner, I help clear our plates, and we waste no time heading upstairs to his bedroom. Tipsy from the wine, we slam into the hallway walls as we hastily remove the clothes off each other's bodies before reaching the bedroom. I accidently get too eager and bite Xavier's bottom lip. He flinches.

"Ouch!"

He moves away from me momentarily before grabbing my hips once more and resuming kissing. Placing my hands on his bare chest, I feel his warmth and a sudden urge to have him on top of me. With the lights off, we move together as one and fall on the bed. Without bothering to pull back the covers, the desire too intense to stop even for one moment, we make love right then and there. To our disappointment, we only last a few short minutes before we're both left panting, lying on our backs, completely and happily spent.

It's been too long. We aren't used to this anymore. By the end of the weekend, we'll be back to our usual rhythm. For now, I'm perfectly content to snuggle under his arm between his armpit and his chest. There's a perfect crescent dip there where I love to lay my head at night while I fall asleep.

Lying in each other's arms, I feel the slow rise and fall of his chest and know that he's fallen asleep. Shivering slightly, suddenly realizing the cool air of the evening has come to settle all around us, I struggle out of his embrace to slide under the covers. There, warm and toasty, I join him in peaceful slumber.

I'm running so hard that I'm panting, gasping for breath. I hear Xavier screaming my name, but his cry is softened and distant as though it's being filtered through a pillow. My legs hurt and I'm crying. Heavy sobs escape my throat as blood begins to pour out of my mouth.

My lungs are bursting. I can't breathe. Panic settles inside of me; I can feel my heart pounding in my chest as shadows surround me. Everywhere I look is pitch black. I only feel fear and despair. I sense another presence but struggle to identify it. The darkness is somehow worse than seeing it in the light, illuminating every surface and exposing it.

Somehow, I know I'm being held captive here against my will. I'm chained by invisible forces that I can't break free from. My wrists hurt from the tight ropes digging into my skin, pinching it.

I wail and thrash trying to get out of my prison, but weakness overtakes me, and I fall to my knees, bruising the tender skin with the impact. A tingly sensation rushes through my body as I feel myself growing hotter with every passing second.

"Laurel!" I hear Xavier's voice calling me.

It's clearer now somehow. Like his mouth isn't filled with cotton but only soft pasta. I can make out my name and the tone of his voice. He sounds worried. I want to call out to him, but my mouth is taped shut. Everything around me is distorted and blurry. Speckles of light flash on and off in zigzags, my vision covered by a dark curtain.

I blink rapidly to focus my eyes on what's in front of me but can't quite make out the figure, certain that I can see the outline of something far away, like through an old dirty window. I reach out a hand to grasp for it but only feel cold air on my fingertips. When I open up my hands again, they are empty. I sob, feeling an intense grief wash over me. I feel as though I'll never stop crying.

"Laurel! Wake up!" I hear him calling for me again.

I turn, following the voice. Is he on my right? No, he's on my left. I whip around quickly trying to see him. I hit a hard concrete wall, and suddenly, I'm in a maze. There's no way out! I attempt to climb the steep walls but fall down hard, hurting my arm in the process.

Frustrated, I grit my teeth and taste more blood. Why is there so much blood? I spit some out on the ground and try one last time to climb the impossibly tall wall. I fail.

I slump to the ground, defeated.

Soft morning light lands on our bodies, warming my face. Xavier is facing the wall, but one of his arms lies over top of the comforter. I smile as I interlace my fingers inside Xavier's, proceeding to kiss each one of them with soft kisses. He moans and I cuddle his back, tracing my fingers over his warm body, gently massaging him. I glance at the clock. It's nine in the morning. I should get up and get a bit of studying in, but not just yet. I want to enjoy these few moments a little while longer.

My hands find their way down Xavier's back and inch closer to his front where I find what I'm looking for, awake and alert.

"Leave me alone!" he growls in a low, partially muted tone, making me purr in response. I think he's playing coy with me and feeling excitement build up, I begin to stroke him when he abruptly turns around, almost pinning my arm beneath him in the process. Shocked, I quickly retrieve my bent hand and begin massaging my wrist when I see his furious eyes boring into mine.

"I said leave me the fuck alone!" he roars.

"Wow, what the hell?" I sit up straight, pulling the covers over myself as though they will protect me.

I've seen Xavier angry before, but never towards me. He used to get into fights in high school all the time, especially when other guys would flirt with me. He's always been very protective which is why his outburst comes as such a surprise.

"What the fuck, babe?" I say as tears threaten to fall. "I was just rubbing your back and then..." I stop abruptly, suddenly noticing a purple circle around one of his eyes.

I reach out a hand to touch it, to make sure it's real when he slaps it away angrily. The impact stuns me and I yelp in surprise.

"I said don't fucking touch me, alright?" he yells before he violently removes the covers off of us and gets out of bed. I hold my injured hand close to me like a precious porcelain doll I don't want to crack. He's never hit me before. *What's gotten into him? Why is he so mad at me? And how did he get that black eye?*

I have so many questions, but before I can ask them, Xavier turns to face me, the look on his face telling me I'll get answers soon enough, but that asking any questions would be a terrible idea right now. He's a loose cannon, not thinking properly. His emotions are clouding his judgement. I swear his eyes don't even see me anymore—just a threat he needs to extinguish.

He stands there, bare chested and panting angrily, trying to steady his breath. I see angry red claw marks all over the front of his body that strangely resemble tiger scratches. They look painful, and I grimace.

"Don't you have anything you want to say to me?" he demands, spitting words out at me, absolutely livid. There isn't an ounce of compassion or love in his tone, and I feel afraid of him for the first time ever.

When I only stare back silently, not trusting my voice, confused and scared, he rubs a hand through his hair, releasing an animal-like snarl.

"Figures." He scowls and resumes pacing angrily around the room, circling me, trapping me like prey. "You were fucking mental last night!" He slows down his pace as concern briefly flashes over his eyes.

My loving boyfriend is still in there somewhere, but he too is scared. I can see that now. His anger masks it well, is there to intimidate, but underneath all the swearing, the imposing stance, is a little boy who got hurt and who is afraid, just as I am.

Taken aback, I lean against the headboard, still clutching the blanket in my hand, my fingers turning white.

"What do you mean? What happened?" I manage to ask through deep breaths.

Sharply, he gestures to himself as though I should already know. It takes me a moment to realize he means his injuries. My eyes grow wide in panic.

"Wait, what? I did that to you?" I sputter, feeling hot all over. "But how? Why? I don't remember any of this!" I say pleading for forgiveness with my tone. I pull at my hair, feeling muddled. None of this makes any sense. *Why would I hit my boyfriend?*

"Well, you did," he replies, his tone finally calmer.

He sits on the edge of the bed, finally trusting me enough to believe that I won't randomly attack him again.

"I'm so sorry...I really don't know what happened," I offer pathetically, not wanting to meet his eye. I feel so ashamed. How could I have done this to him?

"It was so messed up. You were screaming at the top of your lungs and jumping on the bed. I thought the neighbours were going to call the cops." He rubs his eyes and flinches when he touches his hurt eye.

"We should get some ice for that." I gaze deep into his eyes, trying to be helpful, but he waves my concern away.

I bravely reach for his hand and he doesn't pull away as I place my hand over his. I need to touch him. I can't have him be afraid of me. I didn't do this! That's not who I am!

"How can you not remember? You were awake the whole time. You were going crazy, trying to climb me or something. You punched me like I was some stranger attacking you, and when I tried to hold you back, you almost fell off the bed, but I held on to you. You dug your nails in to stop from falling. Hurt like a bitch." He rubs a finger over the marks to emphasize the point.

"I can't believe I did this to you," I say as tears escape my eyes and land on the sheets beneath me. "I'm so sorry!"

"Look, babe, it's alright." He kisses the top of my forehead. My boyfriend's back. Thank God. I don't think I could stand it if he were mad at me for too long. "But seriously, that was some crazy shit. You should probably call your doctor or something. You know, just in case it's something bad."

"Like what?" I ask him, genuinely searching for an answer. I feel fine. A little tired, but otherwise fine. I don't even remember having any dreams last night. I rub at my temples willing myself to remember, but there's nothing there.

"I don't know. Maybe you're having a breakdown or something, or maybe you ate something bad? Oh God, what if I made you sick at dinner?" His eyes grow wide as he ponders those options, neither sounding good.

"I'm sure your dinner was fine. But you've got me thinking." Biting my lip, I debate telling him about the other night when Nova heard me screaming, the state of my room and the random cut on my forearm.

Not wanting to worry him, but choosing the road of honesty, I mention as casually as possible that a similar thing happened earlier this week. I keep my descriptions of the event short and basic, not wanting him to grow any more concerned than he already is. Maybe hearing that it's happened before will help ease his mind.

It does the opposite.

He flies off the bed, his eyes trained on me, and points to my phone. "Okay, that's not normal Laurel. You need to call your doctor. Now!" He stomps around the bed to grab my phone off the nightstand and begins searching through my contacts for my doctor's phone number. I'm about to tell him she doesn't work on the weekend when he stops scrolling suddenly.

"Who's Brian?" he asks in an indignant tone.

"Brian?" I repeat, not following. Peering over to the small screen in his hand, I realize he's been reading a text from my classmate, Brian Rous. The text was asking questions about the upcoming mid-term and if I'd like to get together with a group at the library this week to study together.

"That's a guy from one of my classes," I explain, feeling increasingly nervous.

"Right," he scoffs at me like I'm an idiot.

"Why are you acting like this? I haven't done anything wrong." I find myself pouting like a little girl. This weekend isn't turning out like I'd imagined.

"Whatever." He hands me my phone and heads for the shower.

I cry into my hands. What the hell is happening to my boyfriend? My life is falling apart.

Deciding I can't spend another minute in here with Xavier acting like this, I scan the room searching for my things and hastily start packing. Struggling to decide if my actions are bordering on insanity, weakness, or bravery, I rely on my gut and hurriedly text my mom to ask her to pick me up. Maybe I'm making a mistake, but Xavier is acting unpredictably, accusing me of things I have no memories of, and he's losing his cool around me. I don't want to be around him right now.

I had plans to go over to my parent's house for dinner tonight, but the way things have been going with Xavier, I don't want to hang around here any longer than I need to.

Leaving the house, I glance back, hesitating. I'm being a coward.

He's overreacting, sure, but after two years, he deserves more than me simply walking out on him without an explanation.

After all, he'd made such an effort last night with his fancy meal. Things got messed up so quickly. I shut my eyes, second-guessing myself for a moment. *I just need a little time*, I decide. A little distance to think things over. This week has thrown me for a loop, and I'm finding it hard to make heads or tails of it.

Climbing into the passenger seat of my mom's SUV, I pull my duffle bag over my knees and lean in to give her a kiss on the cheek. I don't need to make excuses as to why Xavier isn't driving me over like we had planned. She already knows. Mother's intuition or whatever. She can decipher my mood solely by how I'm holding myself. She reads the silence between the words.

"Want to talk about it?" she pries gently, doing her best to keep her face neutral and staring ahead.

"Not really." I exhale loudly. My mom's never been a huge fan of Xavier. She's never said anything outright, but I've always sensed her disapproval of him.

"Alright, hon." She pats my knee gently before adding, "I'm here whenever you want to talk." I glance sideways and see a coy smile play on her lips.

"Oh geez, mom. You could at least pretend to be upset for me," I chide her. "Sorry to burst your bubble, but we haven't broken up or anything like that. Just a big fight, that's all." I don't know who I'm trying to convince, my mom or myself.

My mom simply nods and remains quiet, both hands on the wheel as we head back towards town. I stare out my window worried I've just made a grave mistake. Everything has a consequence. What if walking out on Xavier causes an unfixable rift between us? No. I did the right thing. It made no sense to stay over there with him being so livid with me. There was no talking him down. We both need time to cool off. But how much time? How much distance? We already live in different cities. What if we've been apart from each other's daily lives for so long that we just don't know how to be together anymore?

My friends had warned me when I moved away. Long-distance relationships almost never make it. Too much happens every day to share with your partner. At first, you share every joke, discuss every meal in detail, and make an effort to talk on the phone as much as possible.

But as you get more and more accustomed to your new surroundings and make new friends, suddenly, there are more missed calls than actual calls, more vague texts, less detail in conversations, and more excuses to miss events. Weekends go by without hearing from each other until a crater forms in the relationship and one or both partners realize they are fine without the other. My friends had been against my move, afraid it would break Xavier and me up. I'd been defensive, laughing it off.

"That will never happen to us," I'd assured them. Yet here we were. We couldn't take back those days we'd lost or the words we'd spoken to each other this morning. The damage had been done. Could we fix it and move past this? Perhaps, but the hurt would always remain.

The buildings flash by us as we drive past the plethora of semi-detached bungalows lining the edge of town. The old two-story brick-and-mortar homes reserved for downtown living or rented out to business owners for law firms and life insurance companies fence the road, guarding suburbia from the traffic noise. Not that there would be much of that going on here. Old rusty train tracks encircle the outskirts of the countryside, winding their way out towards larger cities.

"Everything okay, hon?" Mom asks me after ten minutes of silence. She's looking at me sideways, her smirk exchanged for creased eyebrows. She's concerned. Finally, she's emitting an appropriate response to the situation.

I'm not generally quiet for very long. I don't know whether it's the side-by-side posture that makes it less intimidating to spill my darkest secrets, or the fact that we can naturally gaze ahead without being rude, but conversation tends to flow more freely for me during car rides.

I've divulged more than my fair share of secrets to my mom over the years, most of them while she chauffeured me from one activity to another. In some ways it was the most quality time we got. It felt safe. Like there was a protective bubble wrapped around the car that kept whatever was said between us free from judgement. As though nothing bad ever happened here. I was free to speak my mind without worrying about repercussions.

"I don't know," I sigh, already knowing I'm going to spill my guts like I always do.

I can't help it. Something about being back home, being driven around town by my mom. I feel like a kid again. A scared kid that needs her mom.

"Something strange has been happening to me, or around me, I'm not sure."

I start babbling and tell her everything that's happened during the last week, starting with Nova's tale of my nightmare. I tell her about my lack of focus, the excessive tiredness, the odd things occurring at the rental house with my food going missing, the shower, and the strange noise in the spare room, finishing with my supposed attack on Xavier and our fight about Brian. I feel fifty pounds lighter when I'm through, but the car feels heavy with all I've released as though all the burdens I've shaken loose are floating around us.

My mom remains quiet, patiently allowing time for any last-minute revelations before she speaks. I'm fully expecting a lecture from her, but what she says surprises me. Not only does she not say what I'm expecting—that Xavier is bad for me and I can do better; that I work too much or too hard; that I need more sleep; that I should try to add more greens to my meals—but she also doesn't seem at all surprised by my tale.

She's the epitome of calm.

She doesn't act shocked to hear about how I destroyed the room she only recently helped me decorate, or how I hurt my boyfriend. Instead, she tells me a story about when I was three years old.

"You used to have night terrors then," she explains as we pull into my parents' driveway.

We sit there unmoving, as the low rumble of the car idling almost lulls me to sleep. She tells me how I used to scream bloody murder every single night for months, and about how I would stand on the bed, drenched in sweat, and attack my parents whenever they tried to intervene. Apparently, I could have had a professional career as a kickboxer based on how many times I'd drop-kicked them in the shins. As a child, I'd used any means necessary to protect myself during these "episodes," as Mom calls them. I'd bitten them, scratched them, pulled on their clothes and hair, and thrown whatever objects I could get my hands on at them.

"See this?" She lifts the sleeve on her jacket to reveal a crescent moon-shaped white line on the inside of her arm, an old scar she'd always told me she'd gotten from a sharp metal ridge while opening a can of beans. "This is just one of the times I got a little too close to you while you had one of your episodes." She laughs, but I stare at her bewildered.

How can she make light of this? I'd permanently injured my own mother at three years old. I'm a monster. I have no words as the shock of her revelation seems to steal the breath from my lungs. Car talks were helpful for me to share hidden secrets, but it never occurred to me until now that my mother could use this sacred space as her own confessional.

"Your eyes would be wide open," she continues. "You looked like you were awake, but you weren't." She sighs, obviously reliving the memory of it. "Believe me. You weren't there. It's like you were possessed by demons or something." She chuckles at her bad joke. "We even debated calling a priest to perform an exorcism," she goes on, before her face grows suddenly serious. "It was absolutely horrifying to watch. There was literally nothing we could do to help you or keep you from hurting yourself, or us. We didn't know how to make the night terrors stop."

"How did they stop, then?" I ask her, waiting expectantly for a magical cure to my current reality.

"Eventually, you just grew out of them, I suppose." She smiles, but worry is etched on her face. She passes a hand over my cheek. "Don't worry, hon, it'll be okay." She tries to sound reassuring, but her eye twitches as the trauma I caused her back in the day resurfaces. I survey my hands, wondering how these little fingers could have caused so much damage.

"I'll phone Dr. Harold once we get inside and request a sleep study," my mother declares, taking charge.

There's no point in arguing with her. Once she makes her mind up about something, it's as good as done. Decidedly, and to prove that the conversation is over, she shuts off the engine, opens her car door, and steps out into the blistering wind.

The weather seems to be cooling down quicker around these parts. Fall always seems a step ahead in this town. Part of the charm, I guess. The leaves tend to transform and dress in colourful coats here first. Or there isn't much else around to distract us from noticing the subtle changes, unlike in the larger cities where nothing ever stands still long enough to be noticed.

Following Mom's example, I step out of the SUV and fall in step behind her, hauling my bag on my shoulder.

"But Mom, Dr. Harold doesn't work on weekends," I begin, but she turns with a sly smile.

"Don't worry, hon. Julianna and I go way back. I used to teach her kids, remember? I know her home phone number. She'll have the request filled in before you head back to town tomorrow."

She winks at me, proud of herself for her connections. Some would call it borderline blackmail, or abuse of power, but not my mother. To her, it comes with the territory of being a teacher, of knowing things and people—it's simply the privilege of living in a small town where everyone knows each other and can call on each other at the drop of a hat. The ease with which she declares this, so sure of herself, so confident, helps me relax somewhat. She's in control now. I've released this beast into her hands and she's managing it for me, calling the shots, mothering me. I hadn't come here to be mothered, but that appears to be exactly what I needed.

In the past, the effortlessness with which she was apt to call in favours from neighbours used to embarrass and irritate me, but now I'm nothing but grateful. I'll be getting answers soon.

CHAPTER 9

True to her word, my mom proudly handed me the requisition form from Dr. Harold earlier this morning before we set off for the bus station. She'd insisted on driving me, but I had other plans.

I made sure to get to the station half an hour before the first scheduled bus was due to arrive. Xavier had agreed to meet me there before I went back to Ottawa. In his text, it was clear he'd been furious about how I'd ditched him, but after a few exchanges, he'd quickly come around, acknowledging his own mistakes and profusely apologizing for his harsh behaviour the day before.

I asked him to meet me at the bus station before I left because we didn't know when we'd be able to see each other again in person. That, and because I'm still crazy in love with him. I can't help the way my body reacts to him.

Watching him climb out of his car slowly, one leg at a time, he walks tentatively over to me, like a puppy with its tail between its legs, my heart sinks a little. My earlier anger subsides slightly. I want to rush over to him and wrap my arms around his neck so he can swoop me up like he usually does, but I remain still.

I miss his touch and his kisses. I want to feel his warmth and how we fit so well together. And yet, I stay planted in place, refusing or unable to move, I'm not entirely certain what to do next.

This wasn't like any of our other fights.

This one had been more intense. We are adults now. He'd really hurt me, both emotionally and physically. I'd hurt him too, but not on purpose. We were both to blame for this situation. From this point on, it was inevitable that things between us would be different. We'd be walking on eggshells around each other. I'm not sure I'm up for that.

And yet, our past years together make me want to stick it out a little while longer. What's a tiny bump in the road when you've been together for two years? Surely we can get through this. Maybe we're just in a rough patch.

I've heard that can happen after couples had been together for a while. We are both independent individuals, both evolving at our own paces. We probably just need a break. A few weeks on our own to reevaluate where we are going. Waiting until the other catches up.

"Hi," I say with a silly wave as he gets close enough for me to reach out and touch him. It feels awkward not to do so, but touching him also feels wrong. Uncertainty makes us stay a few feet away from one another. I can tell he's nervous as well and unsure about what I'm about to say. From his appearance, I don't think he slept much last night. I feel bad for making him imagine the worst.

I hadn't exactly planned everything when I made my escape from his place, but I'm glad to see he's taking the situation seriously. Hopefully, it's clear to him now that I won't stand for him acting like he did yesterday. He can't treat me like that—just shove me aside and hurt me—and expect things to go back to normal, assume that I'll get over it, and pretend it never happened. As though I'd ever be okay with how he rejected me. With the anger in his eyes, and the hatred towards me when I'd touched him.

"Hey," he says looking anywhere but into my eyes. He's ashamed or being defiant. I can't really tell. His posture isn't threatening, so I go on with why I've asked him to meet me here.

"I've been thinking," I start, unsure of how to explain myself. I hesitate and bite my lower lip as I try to formulate my thoughts into coherent words. "This weekend was rough...on both of us." He nods, agreeing with me, still not meeting my eyes. "I hadn't seen you in a while and it was hard to have things go so badly so quickly. I really didn't mean to hurt you. I don't even remember doing it. I'm sorry." It's my turn to look down. "My mom says that when I was a kid, I used to get these awful night terrors." I glance up to make sure he's listening. This seems to get his attention.

"Doesn't that just happen to kids?" he asks. I hadn't realized he knew what they were.

"Yeah, mostly. But I looked it up and I guess two percent of adults can get them, so..." I hesitate. I'd spent most of the evening researching on my phone, trying to find more information about this condition. "Anyway, mom got me a requisition from my doctor and I'm waiting for a call from a sleep clinic to get a study done." I grimace.

"A study? Like an experiment?" he asks.

"No, more like an observation. A nurse is going to watch me sleep and see if there's anything wrong with me," I explain generally.

I don't really know what I'm in for yet. Unfamiliar with the process, I'm quite nervous about the whole ordeal, but I pass it off as being no big deal. I don't want Xavier to think of me as weak or scared.

"Alright," he offers finally. "What about us? Are we okay?" he asks, his scrutinizing stare boring right into my eyes, the question heavy with worry.

I can't help but feel slightly relieved that he still cares. Of course, I want him to care and not cast me away like I'm just his crazy girlfriend. It gives me hope that we might survive this—if we want to continue it, that is.

"Yeah, I think so." Pausing to free a strand of hair that got stuck in my lip-gloss with a gust of wind, I continue, "I just think we should take some time, a week or two, to think things over, you know?" I struggle to get it out, and breathe out when I'm done.

There, I did it.

His head jerks up, visibly hurt by what I'm suggesting.

"You want to break-up?" he says through clenched teeth, his tone bordering on anger.

"No, that's not at all what I'm saying. I just feel like maybe we need a cool-down period. Away from each other. A chance to calm down before we see or talk to each other again."

He looks like he either wants to cry or punch something. I force myself to remain still and not step back like I instinctively want to.

"Alright," he finally responds through clenched teeth. "Fine, if that's what you want."

"It is," I say, feeling relieved. This could have gone way worse.

Just then, I hear the exhaust sound of a big motor and spot my bus rounding the corner of the mall, heading right for my stop.

"Well, that's me." I gesture vaguely at the bus and turn to face him. "I guess, I'll talk to you soon, then?" I add, hopeful.

"Yeah." He lifts his chin, his jaw tight. "Speak soon."

And with that, he turns and walks back to his car, kicking a few rocks on the way. I've never seen Xavier cry, but I think I just came close.

Stepping onto the bus, I feel a heaviness within my chest. Somehow, I know things will never be the same, no matter what happens from this point on.

CHAPTER 10

Back in my room, I immediately begin the grueling work of studying for my upcoming mid-terms. I sprawl over my bed in a sea of open manuals, printed power-point presentations, and my handwritten notes lying haphazardly in a circle all around me. It's organized in my mind, but to anyone who might walk in and see it, my set up would send them for a loop.

About two hours into my revisions, I hear the front door bang open abruptly. Startled, I bolt up from my hunched position, my back protesting in response to the sudden movement. I haven't moved an inch since I sat down. It's clear now that I should have. Moaning, I rub my back to massage the tense area, attempting to release some of the pressure and work at the knot there.

Closing my eyes as I work on the stiff spot, I try to remember the unit I was working on before the interruption. I open my eyes again to scan the documents before me only to notice a long pen gash through most of my notes from when the slamming door scared me.

"Damn it!" I mutter, annoyed. "Just as well. I'm not going to pass this one anyway." I have just begun to beat myself up when I hear heavy steps coming upstairs.

I sense my back tensing up once more. With my eyes trained on the door, I see it shake slightly as another door is opened down the hall, changing the current of air.

Someone is upstairs with me, but it doesn't sound like Nova's usually light feet. I'm about to peer out of my door, when I hear high-pitched, girly giggling which I automatically assume belongs to Nova. I exhale slightly.

So, she's brought a boy home, I laugh to myself. It's about time! This must be why I haven't been seeing her around much these days. I can't help but wonder why she hasn't told me about her latest flame.

Frowning, I decide to appease my curiosity and open my door carefully, only an inch or so, just enough to peek through the crack to get a better sense of what's going on.

To my surprise, the girl is not Nova at all, but some random red-haired chick with mermaid-length hair that I've never met. The mermaid and her *Prince Eric* pass quickly in front of me and I hold my breath, terrified they'll see me. I rush to shut the door with the expert precision of a brain surgeon, doing my best not to make any noise, hiding my presence.

The couple enters the room next to mine and I hear their laughter through the thin walls. My posters and picture frames shake slightly as they stomp around next door. *What the hell? Who are they? What are they doing here? How did they even get in?*

I'm starting to freak out. Feeling trapped in my own room, I have a sudden urge to pee. *Of course, I would need to go now!* I growl internally.

Stepping lightly, I make my way back to my island of a bed and shuffle some papers quietly as I try to locate my phone. I type so fast that my phone barely registers the letters but autocorrect takes over.

Nova, call he cops! Ther's too random people here! Help!

Without bothering to re-read the message first, I press send and stare at the phone, willing the urgency I'm feeling to somehow send a sort of telepathic signal to Nova and make her check her phone at this exact moment.

To my shock, it works. Her reply comes almost immediately as though she's been waiting by her phone expecting my text.

All good Laurel, they're friends of mine.

I'm not thrilled by her answer since she's not here to keep them away from my stuff, not to mention the invasion of privacy I suddenly feel at having to share a wall and a bathroom with strangers. I don't reply out of spite. I'll just stay in my room until I don't hear any more noise.

I return my attention to my studies, but I find I'm too distracted for anything to sink in. After rereading the same notes twenty-some times, I give up altogether, gather my notes in a bundle, and place them on the desk.

It's useless. I'm not able to focus today. After the screwed-up weekend with Xavier and this unexpected turn of events, I'm itching to turn up the music on my computer and start sketching a new piece. Maybe that's exactly what I should do.

Clearing some space on my desk, I reach for my sketch pad. Choosing my best soulful alternative playlist, I plug in my earphones to be polite to my new housemates who seem to be enjoying the new room. Pulling out the charcoal pencils from my case, I lay them beside my sketch pad. Flipping the pages to find a blank one on which to begin this new piece, I realize that I haven't drawn anything since the mystery woman.

Clutching the pages in my hands, I'm overcome by an urge to draw her again, but I push it back. No, I don't want to. I'll draw anything else, anyone else. My mind coming up blank, I see my phone resting next to me on the desk. I shrug and decide to draw a portrait of Nova.

After several attempts of tracing the outline of her face, I just can't seem to get it quite right. I'm starting to feel irritated. My usual escape is proving to be more frustrating than what I was mad about to begin with.

Turning the page sharply, I almost rip it out of the spiral rings, but catch myself. I never rip out any pages. It's this unwritten rule I have when it comes to drawing. I believe there's lessons learned from each and every piece. It's a chance to see progress made, improvements with every drawing. If I only focus on my best pieces, I'll forget how much work it took to get there. I'll forget about where I started, the skill and time it requires to achieve realistic portraits like this.

Before I realize what I'm doing, I'm eagerly shading the top of the page, using consistent pressure to create a dark background. The rest of the drawing is made up of non-descriptive, disconnected items.

I have no idea why I'm drawing these images, but I allow my hands to fly across the page. It gives me a sense of purpose, control, and freedom. It's liberating to let something out that I've been holding inside of me. Something so consuming that's been holding me back, affecting my relationships and focus. I usually sleep like a baby after a sketch this emotionally draining.

An hour later, I stare at the page in horror. It's the most realistic portrait I've ever done. I should feel proud, but instead, I'm terrified. The same haunting dark eyes, that menacing snarl, and a smirk, seemingly telling me something I should already know.

I can't figure out why I keep obsessively drawing this woman who resembles me so much. Is she my alter ego? I've heard of those things. Is she a dead relative set on sharing a message from beyond the grave? Why is she coming to me? Have I upset her in some way? Or perhaps I'm more like her than any other relative, which is why she picked me. Or maybe I've made her up entirely? Does she represent something that's happened in my past? Or something that's coming?

Whatever the reason for her visits, I'm not sure I want to find out.

CHAPTER 11

Walking from my Concept Sketching class to the Innovative Strategies classroom, my phone begins to vibrate in the back pocket of my jeans.

"Booty call," laughs Tee as she sees me reaching for the phone.

It's been really nice to have more time to focus on my studies and not worry so much about Xavier. It's been over a week since we last spoke, so I'm half expecting his voice on the other end of the line when I answer. But it's not him. I'm not surprised to feel a little disappointed.

"Hi, is this Laurel Gervais?" a polite but firm voice asks through the speaker.

"Yes, this is she," I reply, lifting the phone from my ear to peek at the caller ID. I don't recognize the number, so I press it back to my ear to make sure I don't miss anything.

"My name is Liz, and I'm calling from Salter Square Sleep Clinic. The office of Dr. Harold called us to book a sleep study with you. Normally there's a long waiting list for this, but after speaking to your doctor about some of the symptoms you've been experiencing, we'd like to see you as soon as possible."

"Okay," I begin, but she cuts me off.

"We've had a cancellation for next week, Thursday night. Does that work for you?"

"Um..." I hesitate, thinking about my mid-term schedule coming up. "I think I've got an exam on Friday morning that week," I begin, but she cuts me off again.

"That shouldn't be a problem," she assures me with a cold, curt voice. "Our technologist will wake you up at six a.m., leaving you plenty of time to get to your exam.

Unsure, but feeling slightly bullied into making a fast decision, I agree and book the slot. I want this sleep issue dealt with as fast as possible. Dr. Harold had relayed to my mom that it could take six months or more before getting an appointment at the sleep clinic. I was incredibly lucky to get in so quickly. I would just have to study my ass off until I got to the clinic and hope most of the material would seep into my brain as I slept. Maybe leaving a textbook on the night table beside me would help the information leap from the pages into my brain. Learning by osmosis or something like that.

"Great! We're located on Trevik Avenue. It's an old building just a little ways off the road. You can park in the clinic's few visitor parking spots out front for a fee of $5 for the night, or if you prefer, you can take bus route 27 to get to the end of the road, and walk a few minutes to reach the clinic," I hear her recite the information by heart, no passion behind the words whatsoever. Either Liz has been working at the sleep clinic for too long, or she was bored out of her mind.

"You may bring your own pillow, a book, and any toiletries you might need. Please wear long pajama pants and bring any personal items you need for a shower in the morning to remove any leftover glue from the probes we'll affix to your scalp. The technologist will explain things in more detail when you arrive to your appointment. We'll see you next Thursday." And without waiting for a reply, she hangs up.

I must have had a strange look on my face because Tee stares at me waiting for an explanation.

"What the heck was that about?" she asks, her curiosity winning over.

"Oh, nothing," I reply, entering the date on my phone calendar. "I have to go to a sleep clinic next week to see if anything's wrong with how I sleep," I mention casually. "Do you know where Trevik Avenue is?"

"Yeah, it's super close to here actually. Just a block or so away from the college."

We resume walking to class when she asks, "So what's wrong with you?"

I love Tee. She simply has a way with words. She's been such a good friend to me, always honest. Blatantly direct, sure, but she's loyal. It's hard to believe we just met a few months ago. It feels like we've been friends for years.

I touch my nose ring, absentmindedly; the question makes me slightly uncomfortable. I laugh lightly.

"Honestly, I'm not sure. Like I told you before, I've been having nightmares lately, and I guess I'm doing some weird things while I'm asleep."

"Sounds kinky," she laughs. "What kind of weird things?" she adds, winking at me.

"Oh geez, nothing like that!" Laughing, I shove her lightly with my shoulder. "No, it turns out I'm a violent sleeper." I chance a sideways glance in her direction, trying to gauge her reaction.

She only puckers her lips in surprise, and nods.

"Well, I guess it'll be good to get that checked out," she finally says.

That's why I like Tee. She makes me laugh, but when things get serious, she's there for me too.

We get to class, find our seats, and settle in for the long lecture ahead. The whiteboard is already filled with important information and without speaking another word, we both begin to furiously copy the notes into our notebooks to study later on.

Tee will make a fantastic graphic designer someday. She's already got some freelance contracts with a few local photographers, creating logos for them. She could do this in her sleep. It's clearly a passion for her and comes as second nature. She basically knows everything already, has spent many years sifting through catalogues, books and any free educational videos she could browse. She's only doing this program because she started noticing she was losing potential clients because some people were hesitant to hire her without having the certificate to back up her experience. She barely has to study and is still passing with flying colours.

It's hard for me not to get envious of her sometimes, with how hard I need to work to get even half the marks she gets. But I can't help but admire her raw talent.

She's an artist through and through. I can learn a lot from her. She's helped me out a few times navigating the computer applications we use in class when the teacher's explanation was simply too quick for me.

My learning disability has presented itself a few times since the beginning of term, but I've been able to mask it by taking copious amounts of notes, relying on YouTube tutorials, and making several late-night calls to Tee for clarification. So far, anyone looking at me wouldn't notice I'm struggling in the program. I'm hoping to keep it that way.

Today I'm working on the computer between Tee and Brian. The three of us have gotten pretty close lately. Since I'm not always texting with Xavier, I've had more time to socialize with the friends in my classes. We're all in the same study group and have many classes together.

Brian's a really nice, quiet type of guy. He keeps to himself and is incredibly talented in Photoshop and Illustrator. It's taken me months to see it, but I'm starting to understand that Tee is into him. I've seen her tuck her hair behind her ears and she has a sparkle in her eyes when she talks to him. She knows how to work the software but is always asking him for help, and she talks about him a lot whenever he's just out of earshot. I'm surprised I hadn't noticed it before. I've really been living in my own little Xavier bubble.

Watching my friends converse happily, my presence in the room soon forgotten, I'm beginning to feel like a third wheel. It's obvious they're into each other. They might just need me to get out of the way. I make a mental note to give Brian and Tee some time alone soon.

CHAPTER 12

The next week flies by so fast that I wonder if time has been speeding up, making it impossible for me to catch up on my mounting list of assignments.

In college, mid-terms are a mixture of large projects and in-class exams. Every class has a different percentage allotted to the mid-terms, but most are going to account for about 40% of my mark. Each semester is costing me several thousand dollars, so I can't afford to screw up. There's no way I can retake these classes. I have no choice but to pass and finish the program. If I don't, I can kiss my chances of becoming a certified graphic designer goodbye.

I've dedicated all of my spare time between work and college to studying everything I can get my hands on. The fear of getting kicked out of the program is very real to me, and it's a risk I don't want to take. I've been rereading materials, meeting Brian and Tee for more studying, and getting them to grill me whenever possible to ensure I truly understand the material in the hopes that it won't simply evaporate once the exam is over.

I've been so motivated but lately my study time has increased and I haven't been able to work as many shifts. I've had to make do with a lot less money to get me through the week. It hasn't been terrible—most students don't have an extravagant diet—but the lack of proper nutrients is starting to affect me.

Lately, I've been surviving solely on egg noodle packages, mixed with boiling water and salty seasoning that I carry around in an oversized mug as I recite my notes out loud in my room. It wasn't bad the first few days, but now my palate is raw from all the salt and the undercooked noodles rubbing it. I'm seriously craving a fresh plate of fruit, some cheese, and BBQ chicken. Heck, I'd even eat an entire broccoli head right now. I'm that desperate for real food. To say I was disheartened when I couldn't locate my bananas the other day is an understatement.

I need more freshness, more color in my life. All this bland food is making it hard to feel properly nourished and excited about mealtimes. Maybe if I do well on these exams, I'll treat myself to a proper meal.

Walking past the kitchen blowing on my steaming mug of noodles, I climb the steps, walking by Nova's room. I've sort of been avoiding speaking to her lately, as I'm still pretty irritated by the sudden appearance of her so-called friends in the room next to mine. I haven't seen the mermaid or her Prince Eric since that one night, but there have been other strangers since then. The visits are always unexpected, usually different couples laughing and stumbling loudly into the room, with the distinctive sound of the lock clicking into place. And then there's usually silence.

I try not to let it bother me, but I'm finding it extremely disturbing and distracting. So far, I've been aware of at least four different couples that have rendezvoused at our house. I'm usually the only one home when it happens too, which doesn't make me feel very safe. I've been paying close attention to ensure I'm locking the door each and every time I come home, but without fail, these couples come and go in our house like it's a hostel.

When I'm sure no one is there, I pry open the door to catch a glimpse of the unwanted visitors, but their bedroom door remains locked. The outside window is still covered with a sheer curtain, not allowing much opportunity for spying from the ground level. I also can't tell much of what's inside the room by lying flat on my stomach and peering under the crack in the door. I'm desperate for answers and I've got no shame.

The only thing keeping me from banging on Nova's door and demanding real answers is the fact that a fight with my roommate would be even more disruptive than the actual issue at hand. I decide to put off the inevitable conversation until after mid-terms and have made the decision to give notice to the landlords after Christmas time. I can't stand being constantly startled by strange voices and worrying about whether it's safe to come out to use the bathroom. It's too stressful.

Thankfully, I haven't been aware of any new developments with my night terrors. At least, from what I can tell, my room always looks the same when I wake up, which I take as a good sign.

Most of my housemates have been MIA lately. I'm not sure where everyone else has been staying; maybe at their boyfriend's places, or back with their parents during mid-term time perhaps? Who wouldn't love a home-cooked meal from mom and dad while you only need to preoccupy yourself with your studies?

At work, things have picked up too. It's as though the universe concocts a plan each fall to make it a living hell for everyone. Why not have the beginning of classes, then mid-terms, along with a butt-load of holidays with gifts to purchase, a time change, and fucking snow whenever the sky feels like it all at once?

It's like the whole world is conspiring against me. These days there's a constant tension in my chest, a tightness I can't seem to relieve, no matter how many meditation apps I download on my phone. I even tried yoga the other day, but my balance is way off. One position almost had me land head first into my desk, so I gave that up pretty quickly.

I find myself listening to Xavier's music on my laptop and am surprised to realize I've missed him. Or the idea of him, at least. I'm amazed I haven't missed him more in the last few weeks. We used to be inseparable. Before I moved here, that is.

We've texted a few times since our big fight, mostly platonic messages. Just touching base and catching up. Both of us seem to be avoiding the necessary question that will either lead to our relationship's demise or a reunion.

I've let him know about my sleep study tonight, and he seems supportive and eager to hear the results that stem from it. I wonder if the scratches on his torso have healed or if the bruise under his eye has faded to a yellow hue since I've last seen him. We've been avoiding video chats until things settle down a little bit, so I've had to rely on my imagination to fill the gaps.

I'm grateful no one called in sick and that I didn't have to go into work, I'm more than happy to skip the extra cash I would have earned in exchange for a few more hours of studying. Seeing the words blurring before me, I sigh. I definitely could use more time.

The receptionist from the clinic had asked me to show up at nine for my sleep study. I release an audible grunt when I realize the evening has slipped by me once again. Like a thief in the night, time has rushed by me so quickly, I've just missed its dark cloak as it passed by, leaving me empty-handed and short of breath.

I wish I could have more time pouring over my books, but who am I kidding? I could study all night long, up until the very moment I take the exam and still not perform any better. My whole academic career, I'd managed to avoid memorizing historical facts or learning subjects by heart, but I can't get away with that at Carter College.

I'm doomed.

Standing at the bus stop waiting for the bus on Route 27 to arrive, I feel a chill pass through me. Immediately regretting my choice to wear a hoodie rather than a coat, I spend the remaining time waiting at the bus stop debating if I have time to run back to the house to grab a jacket.

I hadn't considered the possibility of being stranded in the freezing cold and had naïvely assumed I wouldn't be waiting long before I got on the bus. Public buses have a tendency to run hot during the fall and winter months, making it almost unbearable to wear a coat once inside. Jumping from one foot to another in a pathetic attempt to get the blood flowing through my body, I try in vain to return some warmth to my extremities.

It feels strange to be out this late on a Thursday night. There's almost no one else outside. The darkness fell hours ago and while I walked to the bus stop, I was able to see—very clearly I may add—into almost every house I walked by. It makes me grimace, thinking of all the times I had unknowingly changed at night in front of my bedroom window which directly faces the street.

As I walked past illuminated windows of couples enjoying a late-night cup of tea, of an old lady reading a book in a comfortable-looking wingback chair beneath a lit stand-up lamp calmly petting her cat, I tried not to dwell on the fact that most of my neighbours had probably seen much more of me than I'd ever realized.

The thought of people watching me change casts a shadow on the recent interaction I've had with the father of three across the parking lot of our street who, upon consideration, might have been more than just a well-meaning, friendly neighbour helping me carry the trash cans to the end of the road. Who knows? He might have been enjoying a private show at my window for months now without me even knowing. I tremble, my embarrassment barely warming my cheeks, feeling exposed beneath my large hoodie.

The stars are shining bright above me, no trace of rain clouds this evening. The moon is bright and full, hanging high in the center of the sky. A full moon. I shiver again. I hug my pillow even closer to my chest. My hands are freezing and I want to stuff them inside the pocket of my hoodie, but then I wouldn't be able to hug my pillow. It's quite the predicament.

In my overnight bag, I've packed one extra shirt and pants, socks, a clean pair of underwear, a toothbrush and toothpaste, some of my course notes, some pens, my sketch pad, an eraser and graphite pencils, along with my phone charger, a hairbrush, small travel-sized shampoo and conditioner bottles and, of course, my bedtime t-shirt and flannel pant pajamas.

I pull my phone out of my jeans pocket and check the time. Two minutes left until the bus is expected to round the corner.

If the bus is early, I'll be on time. If it's on time, I'll be late getting to Salter Square Sleep Clinic. I bite my lip, again faced with the well-known fact that public transportation is unreliable. Rolling my eyes, I catch myself. Or am I to blame for studying too late and taking the last possible bus to get to my appointment?

Playing with fire.

I could have left earlier to ensure I'd be on time, but I'd chosen to cram for a few more minutes and risk being late. So who was more unreliable? The bus or me?

Just then, I spot someone running towards me, he's got his hands in the pocket of his jeans as he jogs half-heartedly towards the bus stop.

I guess I'm more reliable than this guy, I smirk to myself and for a moment, I feel a little better.

CHAPTER 13

The bus drops me off at the corner of Trevik Avenue and Meave St. I'm the only one that steps off.

Planted on the sidewalk, I scan left and right. The streetlight above me doesn't provide any indication as to where I'm supposed to be headed. Completely unhelpful, it simply glares down at me, momentarily blinding me in the darkness, while my eyes blink rapidly trying to adjust. For the tenth time tonight, I pull out my phone and check the address for the clinic. 52 Trevik Avenue. I note the house beside me. Number three.

Great. It's all the way down the street. I've still got a long way to go.

Hoisting my backpack over my shoulders and clutching my pillow, I begin the walk. I'm now five minutes late for my sleep study. I hate being late. It causes me so much anxiety, and still, it keeps happening. Most of the time it's my own damn fault too. Like I'm so nervous about being late that I keep perpetually making myself late. I'm sure a shrink would have a field day with that, uncovering the meaning behind my self-sabotage, but I can't be bothered. I don't have time.

Walking at a quick pace, doing my best to make up the time, I ignore the phone vibrating in my jeans pocket, assuming it's the clinic wondering where I am. If I pause to answer the call, I'll be forced to stop completely to catch my breath in order to speak normally into the phone, thus increasing my tardiness getting to the clinic.

I can't believe how out of shape I am. It's embarrassing. I guess between working and studying, I've completely forgotten to exercise. That will have to change after mid-terms. I'm too young to have the lungs of a sixty-year-old smoker or die of a heart attack.

When I finally reach 52 Trevik, I'm surprised to be only ten minutes late. I walked here a lot quicker than I thought. Focus and the pressure of being late apparently propelled me forward faster than I'd assumed. I stare at the tall building before me, feeling its intimidating presence looming over me, covering me in darkness, its shadow reaching far beyond the place where I stand. The full moon has shifted slightly in the sky and clouds have begun to float in, hiding some of the brighter stars. The threat of rain is underway.

A gust of wind whips at my hair as I walk down the long driveway toward the majestic brown building. Salter Square resembles a manor more than a sleep clinic.

I had imagined a plain, square building with rows of identical windows and lack of personality. I had thought the clinic would resemble doctor offices I've visited in the past, with nubby grey carpet lining every floor, chalky-white walls with blue plastic trim, uncomfortable waiting room chairs, and an antiseptic smell lingering just at mouth level making it suffocating to take a deep breath.

I can't decide if I'm impressed or unsettled by this unconventional clinic space.

From far away, I can see the few parking spots Liz had mentioned when we booked the appointment. The lot sits empty with the exception of two cars parked side by side to the left of the building. Maybe I'm not the only one who's running late tonight, or perhaps most people opted to take the bus to get here to save a few bucks like I did.

The closer I get to the building, the bigger it appears. There are cedar trees lining the pathway to the entrance, and statues of little stone children, standing immobile, planted throughout the garden as though they grew up there as part of the landscape. The vibe they are probably aiming for is to appear luxurious, but I'm just getting creeped out. The closer I get, I realize that what I took for statues of children, are in fact hideous, hunched gargoyles.

The manor is cloaked in darkness save for two exterior sconce lights brightening the front door, guiding the way I must take to enter the building. Dead leaves rustles on the driveway, and I hug my pillow closer to my chest. The full moon shines brightly over me. The earlier comfort its light had provided pales before my eyes as fear creeps in, covering the blackness with a sheen. The rain feels closer now.

I'm not getting the sense that this place is very warm or welcoming. It's been created to intimidate and keep people out. Or maybe keep them in. The windows have iron bars on them. What kind of place is this? I shrink into myself.

The two-story building, imposing and grand, looks solid, like it's stood there for centuries. It reminds me of English castles with its brown stone façade and the array of vertical gridded windowpanes.

From where I stand, I notice none of the windows have curtains. With the lack of window dressings, I would have imagined there would be a complete lack of privacy for the patients, allowing anyone walking by at night to spy inside, just as I was able to with the houses in my neighbourhood. But curiously, I can't make out any details from the interior as only the moon is reflected in the glass. Maybe it would be a different sight should someone turn on a light.

I spot a faint cloud of smoke coming out of the chimney. Maybe I'll finally get to warm up inside. Looking up at the mesmerizing swirls of smoke, I notice how impressively large the roof is, almost a third of the height of the entire building. The vastness of it is intimidating and blocks any sight of the sky, making it dark as ink where I stand.

I peer over my shoulder. I'm already late. Perhaps I should just go back home and forget this whole thing. It's simple really. I could easily turn around and miss my appointment altogether, never have to enter this place. But no, I know I can't do that. I need to get to the bottom of these strange, worrisome nocturnal events. For the sake of my own sanity, I need to figure out the root cause and hopefully get some advice as to how to handle them when they do inevitably happen.

Finding resolve, I walk warily up the wide, concrete steps, pausing before the large knocker on the door. The door itself is impressive with its dark, wood-stained panel design and extra height. The bronze knocker is nailed to the center of it and has the face a grimacing gargoyle on it, mocking me and anyone brave enough to enter.

My upper lip curls as I think about how inappropriate this image is for people like me who come here because of night terrors. I don't want to touch it unless I absolutely need to.

Not finding a doorbell and not sure of the protocol for a clinic where people come to sleep, I try the handle first, but find it's locked. I have no choice but to reach for the knocker, the gargoyle's menacing face intimidating and taunting me. Every instinct tells me to run away, that it's not too late to turn around. Instead, I focus on a cursive engraving just below the offending figure. "S.S." for Salter Square, no doubt. I'm inches away from reaching the knocker when my fingers stop short at the loud crackle of an overhead speaker, which startles me. Frightened but relieved, I wait for someone to speak.

I don't know what I expected, maybe a welcoming committee of some sort, someone to provide orientation to the building. Instead, the door clicks and swings open before me like magic. I hug my pillow as the creepiness keeps growing, unsettling my stomach.

Stepping over the threshold, I feel like I've stepped into one of my favourite childhood movies, *Beauty and the Beast*. The interior of the mansion is dark, and the architecture seems to be a mix of medieval and gothic.

Somehow it feels colder inside the building than it did outside. My teeth chatter as the cold seems to seep in through the thick fabric of my sweatshirt and pierce through my skin, settling into my bones.

Up ahead are two impressive double-helix staircases, twisting on themselves above a hollowed-out core that make me stop in my tracks.

I long to climb those stairs, fully expecting a vastly diverse library to reach up to the ridiculous height of the rooftops. I can't believe this massive, castle-like building is wedged amongst regular homes, just a block from Carter College. It feels like I've stepped back in time.

It must have been built decades ago to spread out on this much acreage and loom this high above the other neighboring buildings. Surely, if it were a newer build, people would have complained about it during the construction. How have I never heard of this place before? As I didn't grow up here, I feel like I've missed an important part of local history along the way.

Carter College should consider including it in their brochure of nearby sites to visit, or at least to be aware of. I feel like an idiot, going to college here, living and working nearby a castle, walking by it on the odd occasion, but never being aware of its presence nestled between the trees at the end of a long, serpent-like, winding driveway, guarded by creepy stone statues. I search my memory for any conversation or written piece I would have come across that had in any small distinct way mentioned this place, but nothing comes to mind.

Maybe the manor isn't something this town is proud of. Maybe the building has a dark past, best left forgotten in the shadows. Perhaps it's being protected by some odd, ancient law, but in reality, most would prefer to see it be demolished. What if something horrible happened here, and its very existence is a constant reminder to the people who live here of a tragedy? I shake my head at the thought. If a place like this had gotten a bad reputation, the place would be an even bigger tourist attraction than if it were simply famous for its architecture.

Looking all around me, I feel my breath catch as I take in the gold-framed paintings that line the various gloomy hallways leading to even murkier wings of the clinic. There is an aura of mystery and eeriness I can't shake off. My hands twitch wanting to draw my surroundings, to try and make some sense of this place, but I refrain from getting distracted. I'm all eyes and ears, completely alert and ready to bolt if anything threatening comes my way. I make a mental note to research more about the building later on.

Stepping further inside the imposing space, I follow the inviting glow of a large, marbled fireplace roaring in the short distance. The logs are hissing and popping, proving to me that there is indeed someone inside the building, at least someone responsible for feeding the fire.

On the upper floor next to the chimney is a balcony with iron spindles and more emptiness. I see no sign of a large bookcase or moving ladder up there. I sigh. It was silly of me to wish this place would be an exact replica of the castle in *Beauty and the Beast*. I should be glad, as this means that surely there is no beast lurking about.

Although the fire is lit, I have yet to see another person in this place. It's like a freaky game of hide and seek in here. I'm expecting someone to come up behind me at any moment. I keep peering over my shoulder, but there's nothing there other than the large door I've just come through moments ago.

The majestic appearance makes it impossible not to stare in awe. The many grand features of this place simply demand attention. Hanging on the walls beside the fireplace are beautiful, old and intricate white-and-blue Victorian tapestries.

Dark navy paint covers the rest of the walls in the entrance and seems to continue up to the second floor following the magnificent staircases as though it might just blend into the night sky.

Next to the front door is a gold-framed sign, welcoming visitors to Salter Square. From the sign and the different room numbers, I can see that several businesses make use of the space during regular working hours. The manor seems to hold large executive conference rooms and offices on the second floor for a few lawyers and private psychologists.

The building also appears to host small weddings on occasion as a wedding planner has left business cards amongst the other business pamphlets placed neatly on a glass table directly beneath the welcome sign. I can imagine how grandiose a place like this would feel as a wedding venue. So majestic and impressive. Elegant, but in a terrifying way. There is certainly enough space to accommodate guests, and there's also a large grand hall for dancing.

Salter Square is therefore a multipurpose manor; a place for regular business during the day, medieval-inspired wedding ceremonies, and a sleep clinic at night.

Right in front of the fireplace sit a pair of matching, dusty rose, velvet plush loveseats with rolled arms and French provincial bronze legs. The loveseats are positioned perfectly for conversing, although, from the looks of it, this place only has use for these on the rarest of occasions.

If I were to attempt to sit on the cushions, I wouldn't be surprised to find myself coughing from dust and debris being released into the air. However immaculately clean they keep the floor from firewood bits and the odd floating ash coming from the fireplace, and the array of people that cross this space on a daily basis, no amount of regular vacuuming can completely remove the tiny molecules of dust imbedded into the loveseat fabric over time.

Standing in front of the fireplace, still clutching my pillow tightly, the heat of the immense fireplace licks at my face, making me step back from the intensity of it. The fireplace mantel is as tall as my head. Horrific images of someone pushing me inside it make me twist around with my back to the fireplace so I can look out into the grand entrance as I wait for someone to come get me.

They obviously know I'm here as someone's let me in. Why aren't they coming to get me? I'd get lost in this gigantic place in mere minutes if I ventured out on my own.

I check my phone for the time and realize that only five minutes have gone by since I arrived, yet it feels like an hour has passed. My cellphone's signal is low—I'm barely getting one bar.

It might drain my battery, but it doesn't matter. I don't expect to be needing my phone much while I'm here. I'm here just for the night, and most of it will be spent sleeping. At least that's the hope. Or rather, should I hope to have a night terror while I'm here? That way, they might actually see what I've been dealing with and offer insight.

I guess the night will go however it's meant to go. I didn't bring my melatonin pills. I want to go to sleep the old-fashioned way and see what happens.

I wouldn't be surprised if patients complained of having more nightmares than normal in this place. The very building seems to be inspired by them, offering enough material to summon dreams when your defenses are low; nightmares that stick with you for a lifetime.

I squeeze my phone tighter. The device is my only connection to the outside world. If I can't reach anyone on the outside, I might start to panic. How dependent I've become on it should probably worry me, but at the moment, I can't be bothered. I'm just grateful I had the foresight to bring along my phone charger cord in case my phone dies, cutting me off from everything I know.

The distinct click-clack of heels on marble grabs my undivided attention. I turn towards the sound and wait. I can only see shadows, blinded by the bright flames warming my backside. I must resemble only a silhouette of myself, dark against the contrast of light framing my entire body. Still momentarily blind, I blink and squint, searching in the darkness as the footsteps stop curtly.

"Hello. You must be Ms. Laurel Gervais." The same authoritative female voice that I recognize as the receptionist who booked me in addresses me from somewhere beyond the shadows, remaining sheltered from view.

"Um, yes, that's me," I reply, my voice low and tense. I feel flustered. Why all the drama?

I will myself to be brave, to step out of the comfort of heat and light, and to walk in small, tentative steps towards the cold voice.

"Nice to meet you. I'm Liz. Welcome to Salter Square." Her robotic voice is less than inviting.

I finally reach where Liz is standing and see a tall, poised, middle-aged woman wearing thick-rimmed glasses and a pencil skirt. With her blond hair up in a tight ballerina bun on the top of her head, she reminds me of my high school librarian. She gives the impression of someone who would run her days on a precise schedule, never deviating from it or it would set everything else off balance.

Her narrow eyes peer at me from just above the rim of her glasses as she observes me. Given the fact that we've only spoken once before on the phone, I wonder if I match how she imagined me to look from just hearing my voice. To me, her appearance fits perfectly with the voice of the lady who took the appointment. Her stare makes me uncomfortable, and I start to sway from one leg to the other, waiting for the next step. She runs the show. That much is clear.

She lets the silence envelop us, letting it settle around us, making a statement.

Liz is clearly a person who values structure and order. My tardiness must have rubbed her the wrong way. It wasn't my intention to start off the night on the wrong foot, although I can't say I'm all that surprised. I tend to get myself in trouble often, whether I mean to or not.

She extends a thin, straight arm to shake my hand. When I do, I'm surprised to find that her grasp is limp and cold, making me cringe as I swallow down the desire to wipe my hand on my jeans.

"Thank you. I'm so sorry I'm late," I add, feeling guilty for my tardiness, suppressing a growing urge to make her like me.

Liz doesn't strike me as someone who goes with the flow. Ignoring my apology altogether, she turns on her heel, beckoning me to follow. Pushing through a set of swinging doors, we step into a smaller room adjacent to the main lobby that appears to be a waiting room. She doesn't speak as we cross the threshold and enter the space.

I scan the space eagerly trying to soak it all in. My fear of getting lost in this place is becoming more of a possibility by the minute. There might be secret passageways or walls that turn out to be doors allowing one privy to their true identity to use them to escape unwanted guests, or to hide out in quiet to read a book. Scanning the space, I feel that this room is more in line with what I expected a sleep clinic to look like.

Dark wood paneling surrounds the perfectly square room. Free of clutter, save for a dozen chairs that sit in the center of the room, perfectly spaced and centered in four neat rows down the middle of the room, like an intimate Weight Watchers' meeting. There are other patients here, and I feel my shoulders relax a little and lessen my grip on my pillow.

How juvenile I feel. As usual, I'd let my imagination get carried away and it had fed my fears with thoughts of this place holding some mysterious and gloomy secret. There are no evil beings looming in the corners, no spiritual forces at work here. Just questionable design, dark wood, and large empty spaces.

The few other people present sitting sporadically on the chairs, glance up simultaneously when Liz walks me through. She indicates that I should sit with a simple nod at a chair.

Without wasting any more time than I already have, I slump into the first seat I see, carefully placing my pillow on my knees and my bag between my feet. I try my best not to make a sound, fearing I may disrupt the library-like silence and create more enemies for myself. The room is so quiet that every tiny noise is amplified.

I turn around to look at the other people and notice a middle-aged woman with wavy, shoulder-length brown hair and thin lips sits a few rows down from me and is yawning steadily, making a breathy sound as she does. Her mouth gapes open so wide, her palm does a terrible job of hiding her large teeth. She reminds me of a horse, and looks like she would be quite content to lie across a few of the chairs for the night and pass out. Her full figure suits her. She seems comfortable in her skin, and sports grey sweatpants and a baby blue sweatshirt. If I'd have to guess, I would say she has a few young kids. I wonder what sleep disorder she has.

Sitting next to her is a man in his thirties who is texting sharply on his phone, almost militarily, sending out commands rather than having a conversation.

He drips of money, looking important in a perfectly tailored business suit, an impressive watch firmly on his wrist, and shiny, dark leather shoes which I'm sure are a high-end brand. He has a slight figure, immaculately neat fingernails, a clean-shaven jaw, and a pointed nose. He's resting one ankle over his opposite knee, jiggling his leg.

I watch, mesmerized, noting his perfectly cropped hair, and see him take a sip from a large cup of coffee. Who drinks coffee at night? I guess people who can't sleep anyway. Either he's had quite a few coffees of late, or he's failing to conceal how nervous he is to be here.

In the back, sitting just below a glowing Exit sign, is a grumpy-looking old man who has his arms folded over a rather bloated belly showing signs of too many years living an unhealthy lifestyle. I wonder if his seating choice was unconscious or deliberate. He looks like he'd rather be anywhere else.

Every once in a while, he releases mucus from his throat and coughs loudly. Even from my position in the front, I can see long untamed, grey nose hairs that beg to be plucked, and nails yellowed from years of smoking cigarettes. He has a comically rounded face, and is slightly balding at the top with only a crown of thinning grey hair. His nose is hooked, and his eyebrows large and untamed. He would be the last picked in a line-up of potential Santa Claus candidates.

Next to the old man, there's a good-looking man in his late fifties. He has short dark hair, dark eyes, and tanned skin. He's wearing only a red t-shirt, as though unaffected by the cold. He sees me looking and smiles back shyly, showing a perfect row of pearly-white teeth.

I turn back towards the front and catch sight of the two men sitting in the row behind mine. One looks to be in his thirties with a small gut hanging over his jeans. He's sitting in similar fashion to the businessman, with his ankle resting over his knee, his back bent, eyes glued to his phone. His sleek black hair is pulled into a man-bun which shakes as he types away on his device enthusiastically. He's got a strange, long-sleeved shirt that is probably in style but looks suspiciously thin like it could tear at any moment. Maybe that's the point.

In his row, two seats down, sitting directly behind me is a man who appears to be in his sixties. He's wearing stylish, thick-rimmed glasses and looking around the room, obviously uncomfortable. I can tell that, like many of us, he hates being here. I also notice he's wearing a gold ring on his left hand. He's probably cruised through life avoiding clinics and doctor offices, downplaying every symptom until his wife said enough was enough.

I wonder if he's ever slept anywhere but in his own bed. Has he ever spent a night away from his wife? Do sleep clinics take that into account? People get used to the warm bodies lying beside them, especially after being married for decades. How would sleeping in a strange clinic without your significant other alter the results of your sleep study? It must take some people a very long time to fall asleep.

I'm nervous about it, but I sleep more on my own than with Xavier, which is why I feel reassured that I'll sleep eventually. My biggest concern is whether or not I'll have a night terror while I'm here. I wish they had a way to monitor sleep patterns at individual homes, in a comfortable, familiar environment. The results would be much more accurate then.

Although, the idea of having a stranger in your house overnight, staring at you while you sleep doesn't feel all that much better. Plus, they already have the perfect set-up here and all the equipment they need. It's much more efficient this way. I understand that, and yet, it doesn't make me feel any better being here.

There are eight patients in total in the waiting room, but only two of us are women. I've read that sleep disorders, especially sleep apnea, majorly affects men, and older men seem to be in the top percentile. If anyone is keeping track of the statistics, I'd say this room is a stellar representation of the article I've read.

Almost everyone is staring at their phone as we wait for Liz to begin, even though most of us can't seem to find any signal. It seems the farther inside the building we get, the worse our Wi-Fi connection gets. So far, I've seen two or three people raise their phones in the air and move it around trying to catch a stronger signal. I have to suppress a giggle. They look like they're at a rock concert, waving a lighter to a slow song.

In my row, there's an attractive young man, about my age, swiping on his phone. At first, I thought he was on a dating app, but then I notice pie chart graphs and long form bullet points which tell me he must be a student as well. Sensing my stare, he looks up and our eyes lock briefly. I inhale quickly.

His eyes are the most beautiful ocean-blue I've ever seen. They draw me in. I feel my eyes grow wide, humiliated to have been caught staring, but he only smiles kindly. He has thick eyebrows, thick, mousy bed-hair, and a subtle stubble on his jaw, making his look distinguished but also damn sexy.

He's wearing dark-washed jeans that are fraying slightly at the bottom, and white sneakers. His black t-shirt fits snug against his toned biceps and broad shoulders. He's got a leather cord bracelet wrapped around his wrist, accentuating the thick veins in his forearms. I also notice a black leather jacket on top of a duffle bag next to him, and a pair of unplugged white earphones resting untangled on top.

He's got a lean body making me think that keeping fit is important to him. He doesn't give off a cocky gym-rat vibe though. Just a serious and focused type. I could easily picture him reading a book on a park bench somewhere. He looks complicated but the good kind. A deep thinker—the silent type.

Raising his eyebrows, slightly amused, he waves at me. To my horror I realize I'm still staring and immediately feel myself growing hot under my hoodie. I look at my hands, trying to seem lost in thought, I absentmindedly grab the booklet on the chair next to me, and leaf through it with laser focus as though it contains the secrets of the universe.

I hear a soft chuckle, but it's not meant to put me down. I can tell he thought it was cute how he had this effect on me. I feel my cheeks flush but also a small smile on my lips. I deliberately choose to ignore him for the rest of the orientation.

Standing at the front of the room, Liz tells us what will be happening during our sleep study. She keeps her explanation general as most of us are here to check different sleep disorders. She broadly describes the layout of Salter Square, making sure to insist we stay in our rooms unless there's an emergency.

The distinctive sound of rain begins to fall over the rooftop, lulling us into slumber, making us all instantly sleepy. The intensity of the rain increases dramatically and without warning. The wind howls and changes direction, forcing the rain against the manor. The harsh downpour hits the windowpanes and distracts me for a moment as I look out to it.

Finding no respite from the cold, the rain seemingly removing any kind of heat I had accumulated from being safely dry and sheltered indoors, I shrink into my hoodie. Willing Liz to speed through her presentation, my eyes feel prickly with irritation. I'm tired.

That's a good sign. Hopefully I'll be able to sleep after all and ignore every gnawing feeling sending my instincts into full-panic mode, forcing me to remain alert and awake all night long. I'm not sure I could handle it. My body craves sleep, despite every warning sounding in my head. I long to hide beneath warm covers.

"Many people are uncomfortable with the idea of being watched while they sleep, but this is a proven way for us to evaluate the extent of your disorders or relate back to the recordings to understand what happened," Liz explains as I zone back in.

Someone coughs behind me, either deliberately or not I can't be sure. I don't dare turn around to find who it was, but my money's on the old man.

"The cameras are strategically hidden in each room. You won't even know they are there." As though this is supposed to sound reassuring. "They are installed for your safety and that of the technologists," she adds before explaining the various sensors that will be monitoring us.

Zoning out once more, I scan the room.

The high ceilings with their dark wood patterns match the large trim around the edges of the room. The room exudes luxury. The lightbulbs are in the shape of lanterns and give off a soft yellow light as though they were actual flames. Not entirely practical or very bright, but they certainly fit in the space.

The rich tones of Persian rugs cover the original hardwood floor, perfectly complimenting the thin, honey-stained oak planks.

Movement to my right makes me turn my head and I realize with astonishment that the rest of the people are now standing and gathering their bags. I've completely missed the instructions, and something tells me there will be no secondary introduction session. I'll simply have to make-do and go with the flow.

Startled, I rise from my seat and throw my backpack strap over my shoulder. Shaking off the sleepy wave that had settled around me, I fall in line behind the others as we exit the waiting room as cattle being led by their master. Edging farther within the bowels of the dark manor, we enter the rest of the clinic, leaving the real world, phone signals, and the makeshift safety of normal life behind.

It should feel reassuring to be surrounded by such an imposingly safe building, but it flirts on the line of oppressive and restricting. Confining and even suffocating. *Is the air pressure different in here? Or is it just my imagination?* I have to remind myself how to breathe normally. It feels like entering another dimension, another world entirely.

Nothing from this place compares to normal life. It's striking, yes, but intimidating and frightening all the same. Which makes me pose the question: what is so scary about finding yourself within the walls of a secure, well-built building? What should bring comfort only brings me the opposite.

As I follow along the line, looking at the bobbing heads of the other patients who will spend the night here, I realize with shock how vulnerable I am.

Why hadn't it occurred to me before?

I don't know any of these people. Who's to say their intentions are good? We are all completely blindly trusting each other, like drivers down the highway. Trusting the other to respect space and follow rules.

What sort of nighttime ailments keep them up at night? And from what I've experienced in myself, I know full well what I'm capable of while asleep. My subconscious has a mind of its own, protecting me or fighting off threats. Whatever the reason, I now know I'm able to inflict real pain and cause true damage.

My skin prickles, the surface covered with goosebumps. Could I be in danger? Or is everyone else in danger of me?

CHAPTER 14

More hideous gargoyles appear on the walls as we make our way down dark hallways, our feet silent against the soft rug stapled to the floor, the velvety red a different shade in the middle than closer to the baseboard due to foot traffic. There are so many different floors in this building that it's difficult to imagine the whole place was built all at once and not extended over time.

I keep forgetting I'm in a sleep clinic and not in a museum. I almost expect to find precious paintings lining the walls, protected by red ropes and a group of school-aged children traversing the hall following a tour guide, whispering and giggling to themselves. Instead, we're just a bunch of tired and disturbed adults dragging our feet until we get to our individually assigned rooms.

A small metallic sign hanging a few feet above us balancing on thin silvery chains from the ceiling indicates that we are now entering the "Polysomnography Sector," the only real indication that this is a sleep clinic.

From the little I've been able to gather, there are no bathrooms in our own prospective rooms. Instead, they are situated down the hall from the bedrooms, one for the men and one for the women. Liz had mentioned that each bathroom holds two stalls, two sinks and two showers.

Instead of a hotel stay, it will be more like a hostel or bed and breakfast situation; not that I mind. I'm elated at the thought of having access to two of each compared to my place where all of the tenants have to take turns with just one.

One by one we are shown to our rooms and told to wait for a technologist to come and hook up the electrodes. My room, door number eight, is the last one down the hall and nearest to the emergency exit staircase. The door shares a wall with a very prominent fire extinguisher that seems heavier than me. It's strange but seeing signs and normal items like a fire extinguisher makes it feel less creepy somehow. It makes the hallway feel like any regular hotel I've stayed at in the past and helps me relax a little bit. The air also feels slightly warmer here as well. I finally begin to loosen my grip on my pillow.

The last one to receive a key, Liz tells me to settle in and that the technologist will be in to see me soon. She lets me know that she is done for the night and that if I require anything, I should ask my assigned technologist or find her in the control room down the hall.

Stepping into my room, I'm surprised to find it so bare. There is only a simply dressed double bed with a taupe duvet, a light wood single night stand, and a short dresser with narrow drawers. No closets or decorations. Next to the bed is a plain chair, similar to the ones in the waiting room, and in front of it, is a cart of multiple coloured wires and other instruments that will soon be attached to me. They seem to be strictly focusing on necessities, nothing more.

It's not meant to be a place that makes you comfortable, one that you want to return to for a holiday. It's a get in-get out kind of room. One you hope never having to use again. It reminds me of a hospital, how cold and uninviting they can be. How plain and lacking personality, as though anyone could stay here. And I guess that's the point. It's about efficiency, not luxury. For a building that oozes personality, it strikes me as odd to find these rooms so bare in comparison.

Looking over my shoulder at the dark hallway, the decor along the walls, I realize that the velvet carpet doesn't extend into the room. The room is designed to look this way, then.

I drop my bag onto the bed and scan the rest of the miniscule room, then turn with the intention of locking the door but realize to my dismay that there is no lock whatsoever. Not even a flimsy chain lock to help my unease. I stare at the space where the lock should be for too long, debating with myself, once again, feeling overwhelmed and unsure about my stay here, in this strange house with strangers, for the night.

It's not that much different than being home, I guess. What with the recent events and the plethora of strangers entering the house at odd hours, my room has remained unlocked since my terrifying episode. But then again, at home I was in familiar settings, this is different. I consider moving the chair to block the door, but rationality wins, and I decide against it.

The staff needs to be able to come in if something happens, and especially to set up the equipment. Dread fills me as I remember the cameras Liz had mentioned; always watching. I should feel relieved knowing I'm being watched by the technologist, dutifully observing me while I sleep, and feel reassured that even though there's no lock, I'll be safe; but I don't. I only feel crawling, intensifying dread.

I begrudgingly begin to remove my things from my pack and am about to undress when I suddenly stop, my shirt halfway up my front, and pull it right back down. Right, the cameras. There is zero privacy in this room. I'll have to get changed into my pajamas in the bathroom stall then.

Feeling like a child at an overnight Brownie's camp, I grab my little pile of clothes along with my toiletries and exit my room on socked feet. My room is the furthest from the bathroom, so I have to walk in front of every room before I reach it. I do my best to walk as stealthy as possible, praying silently that I don't bump into anyone.

On the way, I hear some voices in room three and figure that the technologists must have started making the rounds. There are two of them working tonight, as each room is full, and they must work efficiently to get everyone geared up before the night can begin.

Liz had mentioned earlier during the orientation that the installation of electrode wires can take about forty-five minutes, leaving me plenty of time to change, return to my room and possibly even revise my notes before a technologist gets to me.

Finding the women's bathroom, I push through the door and enter the beautiful space that matches the ornate style of the rest of the manor. The double rectangular sinks are made of white marble resting on dark, wood cabinets. The floors are also made of white marble, and reflect the sparkly light coming off a gold chandelier hanging from the ceiling. The taps and faucets are brushed gold, a modern touch that should feel out of sorts in this space, but somehow works. Circular mirrors with thin gold metal frames hang above each sink at just the right height for me to see my eyes and forehead but not much else.

Looking around, it occurs to me how non-inclusive this bathroom is, with no handicap stall or sink, and no access buttons or ramps to get in. Come to think of it, the entire house is not accessible, with its fabulous stairs reserved only for those that can use them, it makes me wonder how they accommodate someone with physical disabilities, or if they get sent to another sleep clinic.

In the bathroom, I notice that one of the stalls has its door shut. On the corner of the vanity, I spot a pile of clothes. The only other woman here tonight must be using the toilet. I decide to start by washing my face and brush my teeth.

I hear the toilet flush behind me and resume my nighttime routine. I'm just about the spit out the foamy toothpaste into the sink, when I see the sexy guy with the ocean blue eyes from the waiting room, exiting the bathroom stall behind me. He's wearing black and white plaid pajamas; his torso is bare revealing a muscular body as I had guessed earlier—the guy is fit.

I gasp despite myself, surprised to find him standing so close to me and in the women's bathroom.

We remain still, staring at each other in shock, our eyes locked on each other in the reflection of the mirror. My back is to him, but I see his cheeks flush. His mouth unmoving and lips slightly parted, he's lost for words, as his eyes begin to dart the room around for signs to determine who mistakenly entered the wrong bathroom.

My hand is frozen in place in midair, holding my hair out of the spitting zone, my body inclined slightly over the sink, equally in shock. Slowly, I begin to straighten myself, careful to appear cool and collected but my body has other plans. Before I can conceal it, my back muscles spasm in protest to the strange angle I was bent and I yelp.

Toothpaste runs down my chin and I barely manage to wipe it away. Dropping my toothbrush into the sink, it makes a loud clanging noise, breaking the spell we both seem to be under. I grab the vanity for support, my head hangs low as I wait for the spasm to pass. I see stars when I shut my eyes and grit my teeth as the wave of pain passes through me. This hasn't happened in years, why now? Why today?

When I open my eyes again, Mr. Sexy is still there, his thick eyebrows furrowed together, he seems concerned for me.

"Hey, you okay?" he asks finally after waiting a beat, his hand hanging in the air just above my shoulder, debating if he should touch me or not.

Carefully, I turn to face him and find that he's closer than he'd been only moments ago. We're standing so close, I can smell his musky scent, the sweet odor almost makes me lean into him. My right eye twitches and my mouth is gaped open. Snapping my lips together, I feel flustered, like my body has a mind of its own.

I suddenly crave to take a step closer to him, to feel his hands on me. I've never felt an attraction so visceral to another person before. Up this close, I can see a few hairs on his chest, his pecks extremely tight. I want to reach a hand to him and feel his skin, but I catch myself and run my hand through my own hair instead.

I've never been attracted to anyone but Xavier. My boyfriend is hot and turns me on, but this guy is literally making me weak in the knees. I thought that expression was a cliché only found in cheesy romantic novels, but here I am standing awkwardly on two noodles, using the counter as support.

According to his steady breathing and intense stare, the feeling is mutual. I blush, not sure what he could be seeing in me.

"Hi," he says, his stare dances over my face, breaking the silence, a shy smile on his lips.

"Hi," I reply, my voice coming out squeaky. I cough into a fist, feeling out of sorts. Suddenly I'm a teenager again. "Sorry," I say and look away realizing I'd been slowly moving towards him. Swallowing hard, my throat feels very dry.

We both look towards the door, neither of us making a move towards it, we just stare at it.

Finally, he lets out a rich laugh and rubs at his eyes.

"I'm the one who should be sorry," he says, placing a hand over his heart seemingly truly genuine. "I took my contacts off in my room before I came in here with the intention of grabbing my glasses, but I forgot them in my duffle bag when I grabbed my things." Pointing to the pile of clothes I'd spotted when I walked in, I move out of the way so he can grab them.

"It's alright, it happens," I laugh in turn, trying to ignore the nervous energy around us.

"I'm totally blind when I'm not wearing glasses," he laughs, feeling bad for startling me.

He shoves his hands into his pajama pants' pockets, which accentuates his bicep muscles, making him practically irresistible while also making him appear sheepish. He must know the effect he has on me. He's probably very aware of how people view him. But then again, he doesn't give off the vibe of someone too into his looks or cocky. If anything, it's quite the opposite. He genuinely seems nice, which might be contributing to his attractiveness. Shaking my head slightly, I look at the ground momentarily.

This is ridiculous, I scold myself. I need to get it together.

"Really, it's fine." I say and offer a small smile before returning to retrieve my toothbrush to throw it into the trash.

"Sorry about your toothbrush," he adds with a lopsided grin.

"No worries," I wave him off. "It's just a toothbrush."

"Alright, well, again I'm sorry." He nods gallantly. "I'm Roland by the way."

"I'm Laurel." I say timidly.

Gathering his things, I lean with my back to the vanity so that he can get by, and my nose is once again filled with the delicious smell of his body. I feel my eyes closing on their own, breathing it in.

"Good night," he says, and I snap out of it to turn my head towards the door to reply but he's already gone.

"My, oh my," I chant to myself.

My heart flutters in my chest.

I get into a stall, feeling flushed and begin changing into my pajamas. After using the bathroom and washing my hands, I stand by the sink a moment longer, steadying myself before I can exit the room.

I have a feeling I'll be having some good dreams tonight.

CHAPTER 15

Back in my room, I'm having a hard time reviewing my notes. I'm still thinking about Roland, and not feeling guilty about it at all, when I hear a tense knock at the door.

"Hi Laurel, may I come in?" a soft female voice asks.

"Yes, please, come in." I stand up from the bed and move some of my notes around to make a pile on the only dresser.

A lady with a kind face, wearing loose fitting pale green nursing scrubs and white sneakers walks purposefully towards me. Her dry, blond hair looks like it's been bleached too many times.

"Hi, I'm Sadie and I'll be placing the electrodes on you tonight for your sleep study." I nod at her that I understand. "Now, before we begin, do you have any questions or concerns?" I shake my head, eager for this part of the process to be over so I can crawl into bed. She moves closer to me, and I can smell a flowery scent coming off of her. She has large pores on her nose and cheeks, and pencil-drawn eyebrows in a shade much too dark.

The clock on the nightstand indicates it's already 10:30 p.m. I do a terrible job of stifling a yawn, immediately bringing my hand up to cover my gaping mouth.

"Oh, you poor dear," Sadie says amicably, "let's get you settled so that you can go to bed."

Describing the process as she goes, she begins by measuring my head in order to know where to place the electrodes, cleaning specific spots and marking my head as she goes. Sadie then places electrodes on the spots she's marked using a glue she promises will dissolve in the shower. She talks as she works, filling the silence. I'm surprised to realize that I'm nervous, so I try to switch my thoughts from emotional fears to more pragmatic things by asking questions.

"Do you get many night terror patients in here?" I ask, genuinely curious.

"Not very many. It's more common in kids, but they tend to grow out of it." She pauses before adding, "I read your file. That's some pretty serious stuff." Her hands stop, and she looks at me with an expression that could be either intrigue or fear.

"Yeah, I guess so. It only just started a few weeks ago," I offer as an explanation. "It must be from the added stress of my courses or something."

"Maybe, but it is unusual," she replies before resuming her work. "I don't know how much your doctor has told you about night terrors, but they're very rare. Only a small percentage of adults get them. And with yours being violent, it's especially dangerous because most people don't recall experiencing them in the first place." She cocks an eyebrow and looks at me seemingly insinuating something.

"I did read up on that a little bit. It's why I decided to come. I don't want to hurt anyone." My voice dips as I speak, feeling hot with embarrassment. I have nothing to be ashamed of. This is a medical condition. I didn't ask for this. I decide to change tactics.

"Can you tell me more about the different phases of sleep? I remember reading that night terrors tend to occur at a specific stage?"

Inhaling deeply through her nose, Sadie is silent for a moment thinking of how to respond.

"Yes, that's true. What we know is that sleep happens in cycles of about ninety minutes, and that within each cycle there are five stages of sleep. Stage one is light sleep, with slow eye movement. Stage two is when eye movement stops and the brain waves get slower. In stage three, we can see slow brain waves, or delta waves, whereas in stage four, it's almost only delta waves." Pausing to attach a few electrodes, she licks her lips before continuing.

"It can be very hard to wake someone up during stages three and four. These stages are what people refer to as deep sleep. During stage four, there is no eye movement, no muscle activity. Then comes stage five, which you've probably heard of, called REM sleep, or rapid eye movement. This is the stage of sleep where our bodies are practically paralyzed. It can be extremely scary to be woken up during this stage, since you can't move and nothing seems to make sense. Most dreams happen during REM sleep." Sadie stops talking to work on a few sets of electrodes.

"So, are we actually paralyzed or is that just how our brain perceives it?" I ask, forcing the nausea down.

"Well, your body does become paralyzed, at least temporarily. In the clinic we call this stage atonic."

Seeing my shocked expression, she goes on to explain how. "There's an amino acid called glycine that gets released from the brain during REM sleep which causes us to become paralyzed. It's kind of our body's way of ensuring we don't act out our dreams and such. It's meant to protect us from harming ourselves or others, but it's quite scary too. Some research has also found high cortisol levels present during REM sleep, which affects what we dream of and how we remember the dreams." Sadie looks at me for a moment, considering whether to continue.

"Just let me know if I'm boring you to death. I could talk all day about this." She smiles knowingly.

My head is spinning from the flood of information, but it's doing an effective job of keeping my mind occupied while she keeps sticking probes all over me. Her hands work efficiently. She hasn't slowed down much during her explanation. She seems to really enjoy what she does. She's certainly very passionate and well-versed in the subject. I guess that's a relief. At least I'm not getting hooked up to a sleep machine by an amateur. All the more reason to hope to get this resolved in one night.

"No, it's okay. I'm learning a lot," I say to reassure her. "I think I read that night terrors typically happen during REM sleep. Is that right?"

"Yes, that's right. They tend to happen during the slow wave stage, so stage five. Now, while it's mostly kids under twelve that seem to experience these, a small percentage of adults do as well, as you know."

"But why do adults get them? It seems so out of nowhere for me."

"Some people think they can be caused by mental health conditions like depression and anxiety, but it's also possibly associated with trauma or long-term stress. It could be so many things though, from alcohol usage to side effects from medication, or even sleep deprivation. It's not very clear why they happen."

Sadie lets this sit for a while as she continues working on me. She applies electrodes beside my eyes to monitor eye movement and one on my chin to monitor my muscle tone. She fixes more electrodes on my legs before installing a sensor onto my index finger to monitor my oxygen levels. When all that is done, she places another sensor in my nose to measure the air flow from my nose and mouth.

I watch her tiny hands work expertly around my head and try to imagine what I look like at this moment. Before too long, she's done and shutting the lights to my room on her way out.

"Alright, that's it," Sadie says, clasping her hands in finality. "There's a button under the nightstand that you can press if you need any assistance." She notes she'll be down the hall in a small room along with the other technologist, sitting by a wall of computers monitoring all the patients throughout the night. The thought offers little comfort.

With all the wires attached to me, I can't focus on my notes, so after a few minutes, I give up on them altogether and grab my phone instead. I'm glad to see I had the foresight to place it beside me on the night table so I can check social media before falling asleep. It's a bad habit, to scroll on my phone before going to bed, I know this, but it's also not recommended to try new sleep routines during a sleep study, so here I am.

I'm surprised not to have any messages on my phone but notice a missed call from the clinic—the call I'd ignored in my haste to get here. I click on my Instagram icon and pull up the search bar, typing in Roland's name. I manage to find several accounts under that name, but only one seems to fit.

"Well, hello there @rolandrivers013," I smirk to myself. "Found you."

I click triumphantly on the blue follow button, but before I can change my mind, the page changes, leaving only blank squares where pictures usually sit. Refreshing the page does nothing more than cause a buffering ring to appear indicating poor signal. Sighing, I give up and put the phone away. Time to face the inevitable. Might as well try and get some sleep.

As I lie on my side, I suddenly remember that when I sleep on my back, my mouth tends to remain gaped open which makes me recall something from my childhood, how, on average, people swallow eight spiders a year in their sleep. Who knows what kind of gigantic spiders a place like this shelters? I'm pretty sure that this is only a myth, but still. I don't want to take any chances. I shiver and pull the comforter closer to my chin.

I better get to sleep if I'm going to stand any chance of passing my mid-term tomorrow. Hopefully.

I'm on a boat in the middle of the sea. Angry waves move me around the tiny boat so roughly, I think I might capsize. A surfer's dream wave rises in front of me, and I scream. The imposing wall of water is sure to make me fall directly into the depths of the sea.

The ocean rages all around me. The white caps foam as they crash down hard on the navy-blue water. Dusk is fast approaching. I feel a tugging on my leg pulling me under. A sharp pain radiates through my shin, as I begin to sink in the deep, frigid waters. I try to scream, but I've lost my voice. My mouth is open and salty water nearly chokes me to death. I gasp for breath, pushing with my arms and kicking at the water with all my might.

Something, or rather someone is underneath me, pulling hard. A shiver runs down my spine, but not the good kind. I feel someone harshly tugging at my pant leg.

I try to shimmy out of my clothes so that I can free myself and swim away, but strong fingers squeeze my skin tightly grasping my ankle. Again, I try to scream, but I can't. My mouth is full of cotton, my throat is like sandpaper. It hurts so badly, but I'm helpless.

The roar of the sea drowns out my frantic splashing on the surface of the water. As far as I can see, there are no boats, no islands, and no shores. Most importantly, there are no other people here to rescue me. I am alone. How did I end up here?

I feel a sharp tug on my leg again followed by inevitable pain. As a last resort, I dive down and attempt to claw my leg free. My hands meet something hard, not at all what I'd expected. Suddenly, my arm is being jerked back upwards, and my head rises to the surface. I breathe deeply, coughing several times. Blinking, I see the sunrise. How did the night go by so quickly?

I feel a hand on my arm, its grasp tight and firm, immobilizing me in place. My brows raise and pull together as I begin to dart glances around me. I'm no longer in the middle of the ocean but rather in a room.

"Laurel," someone says next to me, their tone calm and firm. "You're safe. It's me, Sadie." Her voice is clipped and effectively bringing me back to the present.

Her monotone voice is such a contrast to the high energy of the ocean that was roaring all around me moments ago. In comparison, Sadie's tone is like a calm lake at sunrise. Her voice makes the dark images falter, scatters them to random places in my mind, where they will retreat until it is safe for them to come out. Her presence in my room should be alarming, but after the fear I've just experienced, I feel so reassured to see her calm demeanor, that I think I might cry.

"It's okay. You're alright." Her tone is gentle as a mother soothing her crying child. "You're at Salter Square Sleep Clinic, here for a sleep study. You've just experienced a night terror." Her composed voice relaxes me, but her grip doesn't let up.

Blinking away through the dark, I begin to see more clearly. I had mistaken her tone for calmness, but in reality, Sadie looks like she's just seen a ghost. She's doing her best to remain calm, but underneath it all, she's freaking out. Her calm exterior is betrayed by her eyes. They are wide and alert as she stares at me intently, as though she's trying to read my thoughts.

"Can you hear me, Laurel?" she asks, waiting patiently, not releasing her hold on my arm.

"Yes, I can," I reply matching her tone. "I'm fine now, thank you," I'm both confused by her reaction and comforted by not being alone.

I glance around the tiny space and realize I've made a mess of things, like at home when Nova found me in the middle of my torn-up bedroom. Slowly, I blink away the sleep and focus on her eyes, centering myself back to the room.

It's a massacre.

My brand-new pillow is shredded, feathers floating around the room and softly lying on the carpeted floor. The headboard is covered in claw marks. Looking at my nails, I see they are brittle and broken—some fingers have blood on them. Most of the wires have been disconnected and hang loosely from my body. Sadie is working on a wire that has wrapped itself around one of my ankles. Finally, I snap out of my trance-like state.

"What happened?" I ask her, alarmed.

"You experienced a night terror," she repeated, this time I register the words.

"Really? Wow!" I say looking around confused. It had felt so real. "I remember snippets of it..." I begin, but she cuts me off.

"Sorry, I had to wake you. We're not really supposed to." She bites her lower lip and looks over her shoulder. I can tell she wants to say more but is debating with herself. A look passes over her face and she resigns herself to staying silent.

"I can't believe I did all of this..." I continue, bewildered. Not that it's the first time I've destroyed a room, but each time it leaves me puzzled. "How is it possible that with my small size and lack of athletic ability I'm capable of this much destruction?"

Looking at her face, I don't know if Sadie has ever witnessed such a mess in her entire career.

"I'm so sorry," I add pathetically. My instinct is to rub at my scalp, to pick at whatever dry skin is stuck there, but when my hand connects with wires, I stop. Focusing instead on the state of the room, I begin to panic. How much was it going to cost me to cover the damages?

Sadie breaks through the spiraling thoughts, placing a gentle hand over mine to bring my attention back.

"You'd be surprised what people can do when they're scared for their lives." Sighing, she begins ushering me back towards the bed.

Bringing a hand to my throat, I suddenly feel parched.

"Excuse me, Sadie, could I please get a glass of water? I completely forgot to grab a bottle from home before coming here tonight."

"Sure, of course," she says, expressionless and looking tired. "Down the hall, past the bathrooms, through the waiting area and the main entrance, there is a kitchen on the far end of the building with a water dispenser and paper cups that you're welcome to use. Just watch your step as the lighting isn't great."

Debating with herself for a moment, she offers, "I could run out and get some for you if you'd like?"

"Oh, no, that's totally fine, a quick walk will be good for me and then I should be able to get right back to sleep." I wave her offer away, doing my best to sound confident and reassuring, but my voice comes out in a hoarse whisper making me sound like a chain-smoker.

"Okay, well the monitor will alert me when you get back to your room, so I'll come and set you back up then." Her tone is impatient, and my throat hurts, so I simply nod.

I see relief in her face as she nods and rushes back out of my room to attend to someone else.

Glad that it seems as though I've only managed to wreck the room and not hurt anyone, I begin to wonder how the night is going for the other patients. Is Mr. Businessman able to sleep after drinking his prestigious coffee? And how is Roland faring tonight? Is he a back sleeper or a side sleeper like me? If we were sleeping in the same bed, would his tall, toned frame envelope mine—big spoon and little spoon?

Shaking my head, I will the thoughts away. This is not appropriate. I have a boyfriend! I take a deep breath and make my way out of my room holding on to the many wires still attached to me and pray I don't run into anyone out for a nightly trip to the bathroom.

Thankfully, there are no mirrors in our bedrooms. I think it would frighten anyone to see themselves looking like this—wires are coming out of my head and my limbs; my hair is in a bird's nest above my head. The sight alone is enough to send anyone to a psych ward.

CHAPTER 16

Walking quietly down the hallway, I feel like an inmate breaking out of jail. I have no idea why I can't remember my dream. Only flashes of images come to mind, but they disappear almost as quickly as they come. I remember that night terrors aren't like nightmares, and one of the main differences is that most people experience amnesia upon waking up, meaning they don't remember anything.

So, in a sense, it's normal for me to not remember shredding an entire room while I slept. Completely normal in fact. Then how come I don't feel reassured about it? And how is it that I remember some parts but not others? Could I be remembering faintly because Sadie woke me in the middle of it? Jarred me from the dream so abruptly that some of it lingered in the air between us for a moment before it drifted off and went where dreams go during the daytime?

I guess we'll never know for certain.

Faint emergency lights illuminate the hallway floors casting strange shadows onto the walls. The gargoyles look even more menacing now than they did earlier. I feel my pace quicken. If I weren't desperate for water, I'd probably turn around right now. I'm such a scaredy-cat. It's embarrassing to admit, but I feel residual fear of the dark from my childhood. Unfortunately, I have no choice. My throat is on fire. I push forward.

The building is eerily quiet. I can hear the change from carpet to hard floor, even though I'm in stockinged feet. The fire has been reduced to an orange glow of hot coals burning in the vast fireplace. Chills course through me, and I hug myself trying my best not to take off in a sprint. Finally, I spot the faint glow of fluorescent lights ahead, a sure sign that I've almost reached the kitchen.

Pushing through double swinging doors, I enter the large kitchen. The light I'd seen is coming from the pantry door left slightly ajar. Maybe someone had visited the kitchen for a midnight snack and left it on. I chuckle to myself at the absurdity of someone scavenging the pantry desperate for food. It's something I would do at home but wouldn't dare to do here in the unknown corners of this place. If it weren't for my dry throat, I would never have ventured away from my room.

On the far wall, I notice an ancient-looking stove, some aluminum pots and pans hanging from the ceiling and, next to a large retro-looking white fridge, the water-cooler.

Pleased to have found it, I reach for a paper cup and fill it up. The cool water rushes down my throat, instantly soothing it. I drain my cup, fill another, and drain it also. My thirst quenched, I crumple the cup in a fist and throw it in a nearby garbage can. Pushing one of the swinging doors, I head back towards my room.

My eyes have a harder time readjusting to the dark now that they've been exposed to light; even the small light from the pantry door is enough to cause my vision to falter. Blinking away the floating spots before my eyes, I use my hands to guide myself along the corridor walls.

Feeling the bumps of the wall molding followed by long stretches of the smooth wood, I feel like a child exploring, using all of my senses to guide me. In a hurry to get back to the makeshift safety of my borrowed bedroom, my pace quickens. I don't waste time, making my way back through the entrance and once again through the waiting area. To my right, I notice an open door.

Light floods through the opening and I can see a lipstick-stained, white ceramic coffee mug next to a computer monitor—Sadie's seat. Above it are dozens of black and white screens, all of them turned on.

There's an empty seat next to Sadie's workstation, and looking at the screens, I see a man in the elderly man's room fixing some device over his face. I've heard sleep apnea is more common in men, especially overweight men, so I'm not at all surprised to see that this man is getting a continuous positive airway pressure (CPAP) machine.

I keep looking at the screens, but I don't see Sadie anywhere. She must be on break.

Lingering at the door, I'm about to step away and move back towards my bedroom when a hand grabs my shoulder and pulls me back immediately covering my mouth.

Too shocked to react, I don't consider grabbing the door frame until I'm too far away to reach it. My hands wave in empty air, and they fail to connect with anything to stop me from being pulled back. Instead, I attempt kicking my feet, but it's useless. Both technologists are busy with other patients, or simply away from their desks. There's no one in the room who can come to my aid.

The hand over my mouth is rough and tight, constricting my airway with a thumb perfectly positioned over my nostrils. My nose ring aches with the pressure. I blink away tears in my eyes and do my best to focus.

Think! I will myself. Remembering a Sandra Bullock movie, I begin to kick behind me and connect with a knee, earning a satisfying grunt from my assailant. The voice is male. Wracking my brain, I try to remember the simple move I'd learned for self-defense in gym class, but my mind comes up blank.

With all the cameras in this place, you'd think someone would see what's happening to me. I'm furious and exhausted. My muscles tense, and I feel a shin splint in one of my legs. I moan as the pain gets worse. It must have been due to my earlier hasty walk while trying to make it here on time. I feel strong arms pulling me backwards. I'm about to use all my strength to connect with the stranger's groin when I hear my attacker speak.

"Shhh!" he begs.

I react by yelling as loudly as I can against his pressed palm but barely any noise comes out. I just end up puffing my cheeks and blocking my ears as the air has nowhere else to go. Frustrated and drained of energy, I make myself limp. I remember seeing something about this on television one night. It makes you harder to manipulate, I believe.

Just as I'd hoped, my attacker stops in his tracks.

"Shit, shit, no! Laurel, please, stop fighting and just come with me!" he pleads, still clutching a palm to my face.

Wait, what? This guy knows my name. And then it dawns on me—the plaid pajamas, the strong grip, and my name on his lips. My attacker is Roland!

I'm frantic. I'd fallen for his trap. Thought he was just a nice guy and, like a fly drawn to honey, I'd let his charm blind me to who he really was. Fuming, I begin thrashing like a fish out of water. I swing my legs and beat at the air with my arms. Finally, I hear his tense voice in my ear. It's so low I have to strain to hear it.

"Laurel, stop, you're okay," his breathing is laboured. "I'm not here to hurt you, I'm trying to save you." This makes me cease all movements.

Save me? Then why did he attack me?

I'd laugh if my mouth were free, but my chest contorts, reminding me that I'm in desperate need of oxygen. I suck in trying to get as much air as I can but only end up sucking his palm. I place my hands over his and begin frantically pulling, trying to communicate my inability to breath.

"Oh, crap! Sorry!" He immediately releases his grip and gently turns me around.

Greedily, I gasp for air, taking in as much as I possibly can. Feeling faint, I lean against the wall for support while grabbing at my chest. My heart is beating so fast! It takes a moment until I regain composure and raise my gaze to meet his.

He looks different than he did when we met in the bathroom, and it takes me a few seconds to realize it's because he's now wearing glasses—like he'd mentioned he needed. Taking in the plain, rumpled sheets and a pile of clothes on the floor, I realize that we're standing in the middle of his room.

Running a hand through his hair, he whispers, "Laurel, I'm so sorry! I was so focused on getting you out of the hallway quietly that I didn't realize I was blocking your airway."

Taking deep breaths, I'm about to begin yelling at him when he raises his hands to stop me, begging me to remain silent. A desperate look appears on his face and it's enough for me to take him seriously. If I calm down, then I might get some answers to explain why he's keeping me as a hostage in his room.

Determined to get answers, I shut my mouth, make my way across the room to sit on his bed, stubbornly cross my legs, and wait for him to speak.

CHAPTER 17

A small smile plays on his lips, and I feel my heart flutter. Damn that smile! Why does my kidnapper have to look so gorgeous?

"Thank you for hearing me out, Laurel," he begins, visibly grateful.

My name on his lips stirs up dormant feelings I'd pushed away over the years—feelings of romance and chivalry. I lick my lips unwillingly, wishing he would come a bit closer so that I could uncross my legs and wrap them around his waist instead.

Jesus, what's wrong with me? I snap out of it. This is wrong on so many levels.

"Okay, okay." He's nervous and in a hurry. I can tell by the slight tremble of his chin and the way he paces agitatedly around the small space. "We don't have much time," he says urgently, grabbing my full attention. For what? I want to ask, but I don't need to.

"This guy, Pete, one of the technologists—the one responsible for the men here—I know him." He pauses, gathering his thoughts, choosing the direction of the conversation. "I don't know how to tell you, so I'll just say it." Taking a deep breath, he exhales slowly, readying himself. "His real name is Troy Robinson. The guy is a pervert, like a legit sex offender." The name rings a bell, but it's only a vague memory.

He stares at me, gauging my reaction. I don't dare flinch or make any movements. There are hundreds of questions bouncing around in my head, but I fear that if I move, I'll destroy this moment and with it, my chance to understand what Roland is telling me.

"He's my friend's older brother. He went to jail for assaulting a girl when I was in high school. You may even have heard about it but it was a few years ago. He got five years. He broke into this girl's dorm room and brutally assaulted her. It was horrible! Somehow, she survived and managed to report him. He went to jail, but recently got out." Rubbing his chin, he waits a beat, turning his head slightly to listen for any noises.

"Look, he can't know you're in here. You should move closer to the door. The cameras are blind in this area here. You'll be safe." He motions to a small triangle slightly to the right of the bedroom door.

How does he know this? I wonder, but I obey him.

Roland takes a few hesitant steps towards me, respectfully maintaining a few feet between us. It's clear that he doesn't want this Troy guy to hear us or to know we're talking.

"Sorry to alarm you like this, and I'm terribly sorry for how it had to happen, but I saw him in your room earlier and I just lost it!" Anger flashes in his eyes. "I don't trust the guy, no matter what his probation officer says. He's not supposed to go anywhere near women, so when I saw him in your room, I freaked out. I thought he was going to attack you. You're exactly his type, too."

Registering his words, I feel my breath catch in my throat. My voice comes out raspy, "Wait, what do you mean he was in my room?" I recoil until my back is flush with the wall, fear and disdain in my tone. "How do you even know this?"

Sighing, Roland looks down at his hands, building up the courage to go on.

"The guy pretended he didn't recognize me when he installed the electrodes on me, but I recognized him. I mean, it's been a while, but I'd kept up to date with his case," he pauses. Swallowing what looks like a hard ball, he adds finally, "I know what he's done. What he's capable of. I know they released him, but he's still the same guy. The same guy he was all those years ago. I don't care what anyone else says. I saw his eyes. It's still all there. That evilness." His eyes tearing up, he looks away.

Confused, I wait him out. I've got nowhere else to be.

"It was my sister he assaulted. Reese. That's her name. He'd beaten her so bad, she barely survived it." He stares deep into my eyes now. "He ruined her life." He shuts his eyes momentarily, fighting against the darkness that looms around him.

"Therapy did nothing. Her self-esteem has been forever destroyed. Reese still can't sleep and can't have a normal relationship with anyone. She doesn't trust anyone anymore, not even me. My sister used to be this free spirit, such a kind soul. Now there's a cloak of darkness that shades everything she sees. Every word she speaks is dripping with fear and anger."

His lip quivers slightly and I want to reach out and offer comfort, but my hands remain slack at my sides.

"That guy is a monster, Laurel." Shaking his head, he stops speaking. "I don't want you to think I'm anything like him, after how I brought you in my room." His eyebrows inch together in worry.

"It's fine," I assure him as I subconsciously pull at my shirt, readjusting it, remembering all the wires still glued to me. Glad I opted to leave my bra on, I feel myself blushing.

"I'm really sorry about what happened to your sister, Roland," I start, hesitant and at a loss for words. "Thank you for telling me. I'm sure that wasn't easy for you to do." He looks up then, meeting my eyes, a tear staining his cheek and he angrily wipes it away.

"I'm sorry. I didn't mean to bring any of this up, but I just wanted to warn you. This guy is dangerous. I have no idea how he's even allowed to be working here. He's obviously got a fake I.D. or something." He leans on the back of the door and pulls out his phone from his back pocket.

"How do you know he was in my room?" I ask again, missing a piece of the puzzle.

"After he hooked up the wires to me, I couldn't fall asleep. I kept thinking about him and I just had to confirm my suspicion. I had to find out if he was Troy. I was about to step out of my room when I hear screaming. When I looked out, I could see it was coming from room eight—your room." Roland stops and takes a deep breath. "I saw him come out of your room, and Sadie met him in the hallway. She was arguing with him, asking him why he'd been in your room. I got so worried that he'd hurt you. Your scream had been like ice in my veins. Pure horror." Roland stares at me for a beat before continuing, as if trying to read me.

"From a slight crack in my door, I watched as Troy made it back to the control room. I waited a minute or two and then I pretended I needed to grab a snack from the kitchen, just so I could walk by. I wanted to take another look at the guy to make sure it was Troy. It's most definitely him. I know now." He sighs. "When Reese was being assaulted, she hit Troy on the back of the head with an alarm clock she kept by her bed. The thing left a gash, and he had to get stitches and everything. It left a pretty large scar." He motions to the location with his index finger, directly behind the left ear.

"I didn't get a good look while he was installing my electrodes since he was facing me the whole time, which I took as a sign that he might have picked up that I recognized him. He's changed quite a bit over the years. He's got a thick beard now; he wears glasses and he's gained, like, thirty pounds. It took me a while, but I'd spent a lot of time around him at my friend's house. I recognized the way he clicked his tongue when he spoke. I didn't want to alert him that I knew who he really was. So that's why I made up being hungry. I wanted to see him from the back. When I walked by, I saw a light, white scar on his scalp and that confirmed it. It's that sleaze ball."

Anger makes his jaw visibly tense up. The muscles bunch up and harden against his cheek bones.

"I knew he'd finished his time, but I thought... I don't know." He stops, lost for words. "I guess part of me wanted him to rot in that prison. I didn't ever want to have to worry about that scum bag being out on the street—having a normal job, a life, possibly even a family—while Reese is still living a shattered life, jumping at every noise, refusing to open herself up to anyone. She can't keep a job, won't go back to her studies..." He clenches his fists, willing himself to remain calm.

"For all intents and purposes, her life ended that day. My sister is gone. This girl that lives with my parents, that's not her anymore." He doesn't cry when he says this. It just is how it is for him. The person she was and the person she is, aren't the same.

I don't want to tell him that most people end up changing or letting us down in one way or another, whether they meant to or not. Change can happen gradually, but it can also happen quickly, in a single moment, searing your skin with the memory, forever a part of you, never the same again.

Feeling the room growing colder, I take in a sharp breath. I'm surprised he's shared this part of his past with me. He must have been truly afraid to speak about this to a complete stranger. Either that or he can sense it somewhere deep within him that he can trust me. That I'm not like everyone else, and that I understand how he might feel torn between the desire for revenge while at the same time wishing for peace and wanting to move on as though nothing's happened.

Looking at him now, I know that he won't ever be able to let this go. Maybe if Troy hadn't crossed paths with him, he could have imagined him living a completely different life, maybe one worse than his sister was surviving. But not after tonight. Roland's sister's life changed that night, all those years ago, but Roland's life was changing now. Tonight. Before me. His eyes glow with the need for justice, to make right what was wrong. To save me because he didn't get to save her.

Maybe it's the sense that he should have been there for her. Perhaps he feels guilty about his absence during the attack. Even though he couldn't have helped, he feels that he should have at least been offered the opportunity. Still, right now he's getting a second chance to make this right. He can stop a crime before it happens. Troy might have paid for the crimes he's done to Roland's sister, but his actions tonight let us know that he's out for more.

He's not nearly done. And for some reason unknown to me, he's chosen me as his next target.

Neither of us has spoken for a few minutes, both lost in our own thoughts. Biting my lower lip, I'm starting to get concerned that I've been in Roland's room for too long. I try to place Troy's face in my mind but come up empty. I don't remember seeing him around the clinic tonight.

When I'd been in the middle of destroying my room and screaming my lungs off, Sadie had come in and claimed I'd had a night terror. Had that really been the case? Or had Troy really been in my room? Had he done something to me? Had Sadie arrived too late?

CHAPTER 18

One thing worries me still. If Sadie caught Troy coming out of my bedroom, then she must have her suspicions. They have strict policies in place here that allow only a female technologist to assist the women and only male technologists to assist the men. So, what was this guy doing in my room?

I remember the cameras and look up around the room. Troy would know exactly where to position himself to avoid getting caught on film. He also would have known from my file that I was at the sleep clinic tonight for night terrors. And as a technologist, he would have known during exactly which phase of sleep it would be best to strike.

I search my memory for my conversation with Sadie earlier about sleep. With there being five stages of sleep and various cycles of sleep per night, night terrors usually happen during the first two hours of sleep. This is usually the deep phase of sleep.

Normally, our body naturally shortens the sleep phases to prepare us to wake up, but during night terrors, we're awoken abruptly from deep sleep. It's almost like being in a coma for weeks and suddenly being shaken awake. I'm surprised to have retained so much information. Perhaps there is some merit to the idea that one has better retention of new material, when learning it right before falling asleep.

Could it be that, or was it just because I then followed it up with an experience, directly applying the information, therefore imprinting it in my brain forever?

I do that a lot.

It's a great way to bypass short-term memory and go directly towards understanding. It feels exciting, almost like playing a risky game with my mind—like cheating the system. If only class lessons would stick like this, I'd be golden.

"Sadie told me I had a night terror," I explain softly, feeling a yawn coming on. "That's why she came in."

Covering my mouth, I yawn deeply, unable to cover it up any longer. It's a terrible reflex of mine, but I tend to get sleepy in tense situations and yawn more often. It's as though my body is trying to preserve itself and tell me to chill out and go to bed to avoid what's scaring me. Play dead, essentially. It hasn't been very useful yet.

"I think you probably did. Troy must have been counting on you getting one so that he could come in and you wouldn't remember any of it," Roland states.

"That's messed up," is all I can say as I try hard to suppress a shiver. "But wait, how do you know about night terrors? I didn't even know they were a thing until I'd had a few."

"My sister's had night terrors ever since the night Troy assaulted her," he looks down, his anger barely contained. "I knew that kind of scream, and that you're not supposed to wake someone up when they're having a night terror."

"But Sadie did..." I begin.

"I know. I think she needed to wake you. She's onto Troy. She must have been watching him on the screen or something. I heard them fighting. Troy knows that Sadie suspects something isn't right. I think she woke you up to save you from him, or to save herself, but then..."

"I got thirsty," I finish for him. "I left my room and went wandering in this creepy building on my own like an idiot." I chide myself.

"You couldn't have known. I'm surprised Sadie didn't go with you, honestly." He shakes his head.

"She kind of left in a hurry actually." I remember now her slight hesitation, and how she darted out of the room.

Unexpectedly, I feel the energy in the room shift.

We both feel it. Like this sixth's sense that's undeniably present. Without saying a word to each other, our eyes tense and we move closer to one another. We just know. Someone is watching us.

We have a pretty good idea who would have an interest in keeping an eye on Roland's room, but does Troy know that I'm here as well? He must see that I'm not back to my room. Is Sadie wondering where I've ended up? How would they handle a person getting lost in this huge building? Would they wake up all the patients? Knock on every door, just to check? Risk the sleep test accuracy and end results, or would they rely solely on the many cameras installed throughout the place to avoid disturbing everyone unnecessarily?

I'm guessing they would choose the latter.

If they play the tapes back, they might even have recorded the moment Roland intercepted me in the hallway. They must know I'm in here.

What's the policy around two patients being in the same room? I'm pretty sure it's frowned upon. I remember reading something as much, in the pamphlet Liz handed me in the waiting room.

Roland looks at me. Something crosses his eyes as he begins to understand.

"Maybe Sadie wanted to call for help? Call the cops on Troy? Or maybe she was afraid he'd run out or hurt someone else at the clinic?" he suggests.

"Maybe." I force my mind to replay the moment Sadie told me to hurry with the water. Had she looked concerned? Adrenaline can make anyone look tense or even in control. It's strange how it makes you brave or makes you act out in ways you never would otherwise. Maybe she thought she could confront Troy and get him arrested.

Reaching for the door, I start to panic. "Roland, if that's true, then Sadie might be in danger. We have to find out if she's alright. If that guy really is Troy, then we need to call someone."

I begin to pull at the door, when Roland stops me with his palm resting against the door and I hear the soft click of the door. Not following, I turn to face him, my face a mixture of fear and bewilderment.

Sighing, he pulls his cell phone from a pocket of his pajamas and turns the screen towards me so that I can see. No signal.

"Shit," I mutter under my breath.

"I noticed my texts weren't going through earlier. I tried to call the police, but the concrete walls and steel roof are the perfect barrier to significantly impact cell signals."

"We need to tell someone." Adamant, I start pacing the room.

Remembering that I'd been scrolling on social media before falling asleep, searching for Roland's profile, I say, "I was able to access the internet from my room earlier. It wasn't working perfectly, but I got through. Maybe we could make it back there and try and call someone? If not, then there has to be a phone somewhere in this building, right? We just need to find it and make the call. But we should probably wake up the other patients and tell them to barricade themselves in their rooms."

Making lists, giving out tasks, that's something I'm good at. Keeping my mind busy when the world around me falls apart into chaos, it's what I do best. I destroy my room because of a night terror? Simple, I just need to run to the store and buy a new pillow. No problem. Some stranger is after me in a creepy manor? All good, I'll just call the cops and sound the alarm. As though it's ever that simple.

Troy might be a loose cannon. Who knows what he's learned during his years in prison or how he's going to act when he realizes we're onto him. The unpredictability of this evening is starting to fray my nerves. It's throwing me off balance, ripping me from every comfort zone I've ever known. I've got nothing solid to stand on. It's like being rocked in a boat on a turbulent sea. It's all I can do to keep my eyes open, looking ahead, doing my best not to puke out the side into the ocean.

"The only phone in this building is in the control room." Roland shows me a picture of the building map on his phone, and I look at him quizzically.

"Pictures still work, but incoming or outgoing doesn't. It's a strange obsession of mine, to photograph the floor plan of places I visit. Just in case there's an emergency or something, then I'll know the way out. I know it's a shitty way to think; always planning for the worst and all that, but it helps me stay calm."

He looks embarrassed at that, but I think it's brilliant.

I can't believe I've never thought of doing this before. Thinking about it now, I feel foolish for always trusting that the people in the building are helpful or kind, that they would show you the way if there was a fire or another emergency. But in chaotic times, people are on their own. A fend for yourself type of thing.

"I think that's so great actually," I reply, and he beams. "I'll probably start doing that myself."

He seems genuinely appreciative of my comment and smiles up at me for a moment.

The moment lasts a few seconds before we look away and pretend to be completely enthralled by the floor plan. I can't help but feel a small smile creep on my lips as we do. I love when people are courageous enough to speak about their quirks and their strange habits out loud. It's what makes us unique, what sets us apart from one another, and sometimes, it can be what we find the most attractive in a person.

Knowing they think the same way you do, that they have these little obsessions they keep secret, just like you. I love getting to know someone so well that they feel completely comfortable being their authentic selves around me, without worrying about being judged.

Thinking about it now, I don't think Xavier and I have that. We're always trying to be our best selves around each other, always putting on a show. There's so much pressure. It's almost like a competition between us to see who can be the most interesting in the couple. I used to think that made us a good couple, always trying hard to keep the other engrossed and attracted. But the look in Roland's eyes right now, like I can see into the very depths of his soul, that's addictive.

I want more of that. I want true surrender, honesty, and nakedness. I want to know him, all of him. The good and the bad. Every scar, every fear, and every hope. Isn't that what getting to know someone entirely is all about? Knowing the ugly but still finding them beautiful. Not about having things in common necessarily, but about a deeper understanding, rooted in place long before meeting. Habits that line up, ideals that mesh together, talking more in silence than with words. It can feel like a string links you together even when you're apart. Appreciating exactly who they are, even if it's different from yourself. In spite of it even.

My heart beats faster in my chest as I begin to visualize myself with this man I've just met. I can see it.

Suddenly, I don't know how I've lived without this kind of connection for so long. Ignorance is bliss, I suppose.

But now that I've experienced this level of intimacy, getting to know someone on such a level, how can I possibly go back to a shallow relationship? How could I be happy with only skimming the surface?

Would Xavier ever open up to me like Roland has in the few moments we've shared together? I feel like I know him better after a few interactions than I know my own boyfriend after two years together.

My eyes are open now, and I don't think they'll ever close again.

CHAPTER 19

We stare at each other for several seconds, our breathing matching. From this close, I can see that his pupils are dilated, making it clear that he feels this intense connection we seem to share as well.

We can't get distracted right now. Our lives might be in danger. We need to come up with a plan to get help and get everyone to safety.

"Laurel," he starts, taking a tentative step towards me.

Wires dangle from his arms and head, matching my own. We look really cute set up like this. It's difficult to ignore all the colourful leads and tape glued to his face, but somehow, I remain focused on his eyes. Even behind the glasses, they draw me in.

Cutting him off, I cough slightly before I suggest that we split up. One of us should try to reach the control room while the other goes to my bedroom to retrieve my phone and call the police.

Bringing us back to the moment and how severe this situation is, he shakes his head, ridding himself of the trance he was in.

"I don't think that's such a good idea. I don't think we should split up." He seems almost pained that I would even suggest it. "We need to stick together."

Roland steps closer again, inches from me now. I have to lift my head slightly to look into his eyes as he looks down into mine. My mind is going crazy, my heart is beating a thousand times a minute. I think he's going to lean in and kiss me, but he reaches behind me to the doorknob.

"Let's try your room first," he says, with a shy smile, as though he's suggesting more. "We might be able to get there before he notices. Assuming he's not waiting outside the door right now."

Just as he's about to turn the knob, a scream pierces the stillness of the room.

We look at each other in alarm.

"What was that?" I say, fear coursing through my body. I feel faint, like my body is shutting down. I'm holding my breath as though it will help me hear the subtle noises all around us and provide a clue of some sort.

"I don't know," he replies, his eyes wide in horror, matching mine. "We better move—quickly." He pries the door open, throwing caution to the wind, ignoring the fact that the scream might simply be a ruse to get us to exit the room, but we're surprised when we find an empty hallway.

A few of the other patients have also opened their doors and are looking out, sleepy confusion in their eyes.

"What's going on?" the businessman asks, taking charge.

"Did everyone hear a scream?" the middle-aged woman inquires.

"What in the bloody hell was that racket?" the old man barks, holding a mask in his hand.

Roland and I stare at each other and peek again down the hall. We seem to have a conversation just with our eyes, quickly considering if we should tell them what we know or not. There's no reason to alarm them and cause a panic if we don't need to. Perhaps the scream was completely justified.

Probably not, though.

One of the patients, the man in his late fifties from Room Two, runs back towards us.

"I just checked the control room, but it's empty," he says, breathing heavily from running up and down the hallway. His palms are up in the air in question and defeat.

"What do you mean, empty?" the middle-aged lady asks, her voice bordering on squeaky. "Where are the technologists?" Panic is settling in as people look around at each other. "What's going on?" She turns, a confused expression forming on her face as she focuses on us. "And what are you doing in his room?" She points a finger at me, chiding me like I'm a child. As though it's any of her business what we were doing. I feel a blush creeping up my neck. Who is she to judge me? She doesn't even know me. I'm about to retort when Roland silences me gently with his raised arm.

"Not worth it. We need to tell them what's going on."

"You're right." I nod in agreement. We don't have time for this.

We briefly explain, keeping our voices low, still unsure where Troy might be hiding, or if he's still in the building at all.

"You're kidding me!" the middle-aged woman gasps at the revelation. "That's horrible! I'm leaving right now!" she announces, promptly returning to her room to pack her stuff.

"Me too," follows the businessman. "I don't have time to deal with this shit."

"What about Sadie?" I pipe in. "Do you think she has time to deal with this shit? She could be injured! She might need help. If you all leave, who's going to help her?" I ask, raising my voice slightly, suddenly outraged at their willingness to turn their backs on this woman who might need help.

"We don't even know if he's done anything to her," the old man pipes in.

"You mean to say that scream we all heard was a scream of passion, then?" Roland scoffs, sarcasm rushing out of him.

We all stand there, staring at each other, daring each other to move.

"Whatever. I'm leaving," the businessman says cowardly. "And you should too. Whatever's going on here doesn't have to implicate us."

The others all seem to agree, and they follow his lead as they rush back inside their bedroom to pack their things. Feeling discouraged, Roland and I look at each other, our stamina and adrenaline declining. We hadn't anticipated that the other patients would bail on us.

If anything, we had desperately clung to the hope that all of us would rally against Troy, and if it came to an epic battle, we would be the dominant force—eight against one. In my mind, Troy didn't stand a chance fighting all of us. But if everyone else left, it would only be Roland and me to confront Troy. And one of us would need to care for Sadie while the other went to get help, assuming she wasn't beyond helping.

My heart beats quickly, and my throat gets dry, as I swallow reflexively. It just doesn't seem feasible. In all of my plans so far, I hadn't ever considered the possibility of losing.

"Please, stay," I beg. "We need your help! We can form groups and stay safer that way." I'm pleading now, really showing my age.

A few of them pause standing like statues, still and unmoving in their door frames. It's almost as though I can see the gears moving in their brains as they mull this over, briefly considering what I've suggested. But, one by one, I see them waver slightly and shake their heads. Not good enough. We have no idea what Troy is planning. Without being able to offer them guaranteed safety, I'm losing them.

With the lights off in the hallway, save for the weak emergency lights lighting the floor, everyone's face is semi-hidden in the shadows. With our monstrous getups—wires, glue, and tape covering our bodies—our sleep deprived forms gently sway from one foot to another in silent rhythm as we try our best to remain awake. We must look like alien creatures lurking around the dark corners of this ancient building rather than the plain humans who entered it only hours ago.

I begin to rip the colourful cords off of my body, starting with the ones hanging from my head and face, resolving that there's no longer a possibility of me completing a sleep test tonight. The entire night has taken a different turn, and there's no way I'm going to be sleeping here tonight.

Roland follows my example and begins removing his leads as well.

We help each other remove some of the more stubborn ones where the glue seems more adhesive, and manage to separate ourselves from the wire prison we were caught in. Lumps of dried glue remain on our heads and rectangles of white where bits of tape were attached to our faces remain, but at least we are free of wires and looking somewhat like our old selves. The thought is both terrifying and reassuring. With the strange appearance, it would be easy to pretend to be someone else. Someone strong, confident, and brave. But now that the wires are removed, I'm reminded of who I really am. Who am I kidding? I'm not a leader! I can't save anyone, especially not myself.

Off in the near distance, a loud bang resounds. Within seconds, everyone is back in their door frames, cautiously peering out towards the direction of the noise, but too afraid to step outside the threshold and into the hallway.

What is it now? Roland and I exchange a look, and without thinking, our bodies inch closer together. Our limp, cold hands find each other in the darkness, and we hold on, grabbing at the other for support.

CHAPTER 20

It's hard to know how you'll react when faced with danger. Some people will have the instinct to hide, or run in the opposite direction, a self-preservation of sorts. Other people, like me as it turns out, will rush towards it.

All of my instincts scream at me from within. I ignore the warning bells, the sounding alarms ringing in my ears, and race towards the lit-up exit sign where the noise originated. My legs protest, still sore from my earlier rush to get to this damned place on time, and from my earlier shin splint episode, but stubbornly, I press on. Despite my growing fear that something horribly sinister has happened here, and my inability to do anything about it, I keep going.

Roland rushes by me, his speed and athletic ability clearly surpassing mine. He and I began racing down the hall the instant we heard the noise. At this very moment, I'm not entirely sure if we're trying to stop Troy from escaping, about to run directly into him, or if we're about to discover someone injured on the other side of the door, but the uncertainty doesn't slow us down one little bit. If anything, it propels us down towards the glowing red light of the exit sign even quicker.

Neither of us are wearing shoes as we thump down the hallway on the old, carpeted floor. Thankfully, the distance isn't too far, and we reach the door, barely out of breath.

The others have chosen to hide in their rooms, or remain by the door frame of their bedrooms, curious, but not brave enough to join us.

With his hand on the door, Roland looks at me for support just as I reach him, slowing down my pace before stopping abruptly right next to him.

"Whatever is behind this door, we're together on this, alright?" he says in a hushed tone.

What does that even mean? I think, but keep it to myself because, on some level, I know exactly what he means. I nod, agreeing wholeheartedly. I trust him completely and I know he feels the same way about me. I can sense it. He has my back and I have his. This shared experience tonight has sealed us together in a way no number of years with someone can.

I briefly consider running to my bedroom to retrieve my cell phone and call the police, but what would I report exactly? That we're pretty sure the man who calls himself Pete is actually Troy Robinson, the man who viciously assaulted a girl six years ago? Would they even believe us? I'm not even sure they'd come over if we told them we heard a scream. They would probably assume we were overreacting. Without proof of any kind, what evidence do we have that something terribly wrong is going on here?

We have no choice but to push through that door to find out what's behind the alarming noises we've been hearing. I look to Roland, agreeing. "Okay, let's do this." I sound like the lead in an action movie but find no comic relief. My heart is pumping so loudly, I can hear it in my ears. Clenching my fists, I swallow hard, trying to keep the fear at bay.

Roland pushes the door open and we step forward into complete darkness as the heavy door closes shut behind us. The emergency lights don't appear to be working in this section of the building. Was that an oversight or on purpose? I can't help but wonder if Troy planned it this way. I'm half expecting to step on some shards of glass from broken lightbulbs.

We don't have the luxury of time to wait until our eyes adjust to the darkness. We push through it, once again, holding hands, our free hands feeling the walls or grabbing on the stair's handrail. We're in this together—a team.

How is it that I've just met this man, but I feel entirely safe in his presence? It's like there's an aura around him, an overwhelming sense of security I can't explain. It's as though I know he would go through amazing lengths to keep me safe. He includes me, doesn't belittle me, and counts on me as much as I rely on him. There's a balance to whatever this is we're doing. An equal respect for each other.

He squeezes my hand as if he's responding to the sentiment. Warmth fills my chest. I feel like I'm cheating on Xavier, which I guess I am, emotionally anyway. I'll have to tell Roland about him soon, before anything else happens. For now, holding hands is innocent enough considering the situation we're in right now. A little act of humanity, offering simple comfort during a time of distress.

I'd be surprised if anyone would judge us for clinging to one another this way, in response to our situation. You can hardly consider this inappropriate behaviour.

I'd like to see how others would react in this kind of situation. I'm sure other people would do some pretty reckless things if faced with life and death hanging in the balance. I don't think many people would blame us for seeking comfort from each other, not when everyone else is seeking shelter, hiding out in their rooms, flat out refusing to get involved in any possible way. At least we're trying to help.

This hand-holding thing could be a sign of support, nothing more. But I know this to be a lie. The sheer fact that I've been trying to justify it to myself for a full minute now seems to contradict my apparent ease with it. The truth is, I'm not as detached and unaffected by his touch as I'd like to believe. It's becoming increasingly harder to ignore the effect his closeness has on me. Because I know I want more than this, and I'm guessing Roland does too. We'll have to talk about all of this once this is over. That is, if we make it through whatever this is.

"Shit, I can't see anything!" Roland grunts. "You?" he asks me, but I'm in the same boat.

"Neither can I. What should we..." I lose my footing and Roland's hand pulls me, as he grabs my arm to prevent me from plummeting down the steep stairs. My arm aches slightly from the sharpness of the fall and Roland's pull, but I'm back on the landing, surprisingly still in one piece.

"Thanks. That was close!" I breathe out, willing my heart to calm down.

"Wait, I think there's something here." Roland is moving his leg back and forth, twisting his body slightly.

I can feel the small pull and loosening of his grip as he moves around, never letting go of my hand. I start moving my foot in a similar way and feel it bump against something soft. A small whimper escapes my lips as I imagine what I've just discovered.

"Oh God, oh God! Roland, I can't look." I turn into his chest and he hugs me tight for a moment, then quickly releases me.

We both know we don't have much time to investigate. The more we know, the better prepared we can be, and the more evidence we'll have for the police.

Finding our way back towards the door leading to the hallway, I hold it open as wide as it will go and fall back against the wall.

CHAPTER 21

A wave of nausea hits me seconds before I feel myself trembling.

My head shakes, willing the images to disappear. If only it were that simple, like when I was a child and I'd shake my Etch A Sketch toy to erase whatever scribble I'd done, before making a new one.

I look over at the exit door, my tongue thick in my mouth. The soft, unidentified thing I'd pressed up against in the staircase hadn't been difficult to figure out. When the faint light from the hallway had shone on it, my fears had been confirmed. Lying still in the darkness of the stairwell is Sadie, my technologist.

My knees go weak and I begin to slide down to the floor. The old carpet isn't plush like I'd first expected, but rather rough and gritty against my hands as they slip over the threads. I run my fingers through the filthy, worn carpet, trying to grab onto something, ignoring the queasiness of touching unidentifiable dirt and circular stains that can only be spotted this close to the floor. Anything to keep me centered and keep me from falling out of consciousness. I'm not sure it's helping. The bile keeps moving up and down my throat, like a roller coaster, playing with my emotions, making me inch closer to the sweet release only to plummet down again and leave me feeling like crap.

"Hey, are you okay?" I hear faintly as I force my eyes open.

Businessman is leaning over me, his brows stitched together in worry. He's keeping his distance as though I'm contagious or something, but he is still concerned about my well-being. He's a wise man. There's no guarantee that I won't puke directly into his face at any moment.

I vaguely notice he's removed all his wires too and has changed back into the suit he was wearing earlier. *He's leaving*, I think to myself as I shakily begin to get back on my feet.

"I think so," I say unconvincingly. "Where's Roland?" I ask looking around frantically. He'd been right next to me a moment ago but is nowhere to be found now.

"The guy you were with?" he inquires, and I nod weakly, closing my eyes for minute to let the nausea pass over me.

"After you yelled and collapsed, he ran to the control room to call for help," the businessman explains, shrugging as he shoves his hands in his pockets, his fists making large bulges in the pressed pants.

"What's your name?" I ask, trying to think of anything else, to fill the awkward space and silence with words rather than feelings.

I see him hesitate, suspicion playing in his gaze for a moment as he assesses me and my reason for asking. He's deciding if revealing his name, his identity, to me, a stranger, is worth the risk.

"Chris," he says finally, hissing the 's' sound at the end as though his own name tastes bad in his mouth.

He seems uncomfortable to be talking to me. Perhaps his suit is only a mask. I feel bad for assuming he'd be something else simply because he was wearing it. As though his having a well-tailored suit made him impenetrable and important, a man who could take control of things, and make them make sense again. He gave the appearance of structure and order.

Perhaps that's what he wanted others to think, to make himself appear to be more than he is. More and more I'm convinced that we work hard to perfect our external images and hope some of it will reflect internally as well as the way others treat our appearance, assuming we are what we portray ourselves to be. If we present ourselves to the world like we have it all together, like we own expensive things and play an important role in society, it might intimidate others, make them treat us with respect, and might cause them to interact differently with us. I wonder what secrets Chris is hiding beneath this make-shift armor.

Looking at him close up, similar to the carpet, his suit isn't as neat as it had appeared. Now that he's standing before me, I notice a faded coffee stain near one of the buttons of his dress shirt, a torn thread loose at the bottom of the shirt that he tried to tuck in but failed to hide, and pants that fit a little too tightly around his thighs.

I feel bad for him, for trying so hard to appear to be something he's not. I just hope this is who he really wants to be and not who he thinks others want him to be. That seems like it would be too much pressure to live up to. Perhaps it would explain his caffeine addiction, and his overcompensating confidence and authority. He wants to be in charge, but when we asked for help, he went and changed; packed to leave. Maybe it's an old habit that's difficult to break.

I stand on shaky legs and look around me. The other patients have emerged from their rooms and all are accounted for except for the other woman who's in Room Five. She could still be in her room, packing to leave, or she could have left already. I turn and step towards her door, when Chris' arm shoots up blocking my way.

"I wouldn't go in there if I were you." He looks down, a solemn look on his face.

Oh shit. I feel a lump in my throat, and I struggle to speak. "Why not?" I croak finally, although it seems futile. His expression tells me everything I need to know.

"When you and Roland were in the stairway, someone attacked her. We think it's the same guy you were talking about. He must have been hiding in her room. We were all back in our rooms and didn't understand what was happening quickly enough." Chris looks down, ashamed.

It's only then that I notice blood on his hands. It hasn't even had time to dry but was smudged beneath his fingernails. He notices me looking and pulls his hands away, tucking them behind his back, but he's too slow. I've already seen.

"I tried to help, but I was too late..." His words hang heavy in the space between us. He doesn't need to say any more. I understand. We stare at each other for a moment before I hear urgent steps coming down the hallway. Roland, returning from the control room, stops short next to me and places a warm hand on my shoulder.

"You alright, Laurel?" He looks deep into my eyes, making sure I'm okay.

Forcing myself to look back, I focus all my attention on him, finding that I'm able to breathe more easily by doing so. He blocks my view of the others a little bit and it helps. For a moment, I can almost pretend to be somewhere else entirely.

I love the way he says my name. The roll of the 'r' sounds both foreign and familiar on his tongue. His presence and touch make my body instantly warm all over. I can feel blood running through my veins, my mind buzzing happily as my fear begins to escape slowly, like a tire leak.

Having Roland beside me calms me. Unlike Chris who radiates nervousness and agitation, as if the coffee he's been drinking is coming out of all his pores and releasing their essence to others, Roland has the opposite effect. Even though Roland doesn't look like he's got it all together, he's the true leader. He takes charge but isn't controlling. He's earned his place because he leads by example. He doesn't throw out commands unless he's willing to do something himself first.

"I'm fine," I say, managing a small smile.

But am I fine? I'm stuck in a creepy manor with a killer on the loose. So far, his two victims have been women. What if I'm next? I feel singled out and I hate it.

"Did you reach the police?" Chris addresses Roland with a note of authority no one has awarded him. Hope drains as quickly as it rushed in as I watch my new friend shake his head soberly.

"The jerk cut the lines before I got there. And since there's no cell signal, we won't be able to reach anyone until we get outside."

As if on cue, Chris and I begin to move towards the entrance doors, but Roland pulls up his hands, stopping us in our tracks.

"All the doors are locked too. I just checked them. Unless there's one I don't know about, it looks like we're stuck here."

Some of the other patients have formed a circle behind us, waiting for news or a plan.

"Hold on," I speak up, feeling a surge of energy suddenly. "I was able to send a text earlier. Maybe it would work again!"

Leaving the rest of the group behind to stew over other helpful ideas, I dart to my room with Roland following close behind. The promise of obtaining a signal is vague and hard to grasp, but it's all we've got. None of us are trained fighters or armed agents. We're simply regular people relying on regular tools to help us escape or to call the people who might stand a chance at saving us. It doesn't feel very triumphant, but that's the least of my worries.

Together, we enter the room and begin scanning it. I rush towards the nightstand, but my cell phone isn't where I left it. Taking a panicked look around, I realize that, in fact, my phone isn't anywhere. It's as though it has vanished into thin air. Troy must have taken it.

Shit! I grit my teeth, frustration building up inside of me. I feel the heat of it creep into my skin. For good measure and as a last resort before calling off our search, I look under the bed and then lift all the covers off, but I can't find it anywhere. I look desperate and I am. That phone was my only hope, my lifeline to the outside world. It's my main go-to when I'm anxious. Usually always available, it's like a part of me is missing. Like a phantom limb, I feel my thumb twitch with the need to brush over the smooth surface of it, calming me down as it normally does.

In defeat, I hurriedly replace the comforter, not bothering to cover the mattress perfectly with it as I normally would. In my haste, I notice my drawing book flipped open to one of my first pieces. The book had been resting on top of the bed and had shifted slightly while I wrestled with the comforter. I lean over with the intention of shutting it and keeping the insight into my private thoughts from the world when I notice Roland frozen in place.

He's speechless and it looks as though he's just seen a ghost. He's staring at my sketch book, his mouth open, his chest heaving hard. I swallow. This is as close as I'll ever get to having a diary. And now this guy I've just met is seeing all my secrets, exposed and naked, laying spread-eagled on the top of the comforter. The book seems to want to be seen, laying it all out for Roland to grasp. It's not that I don't want him to see my sketches. It's just that it takes a lot for me to trust someone enough to share this intimate part of me. I wasn't planning to show him this yet. I'd wanted to hold on to it a little longer, a little tighter. But now that his eyes scan the drawings before him, I feel anxious and expectant.

What does he think? Does he like them? Or does he think it's too childish, amateurish? Part of me thinks that I should feel defiled by someone looking at my sketch book without my permission and, under other circumstances, I might have felt ashamed of my work. But not with him. I find that I'm quite pleased that he's showing such an intense interest in my sketches. In fact, he's probably giving the most attention anyone has ever given to them.

I try to view the book as he does now—a portfolio of hours of work bound together in a neat little package—a glimpse into my life, if you will. These pages contain drawings of people, places, and thoughts, some of which I've never even expressed before, and wouldn't even know how to begin.

The crisp, empty pages are daunting, like a dare for me to use them for my own pleasure, my own need. With that in mind, I shiver. The pages with sketches have smears from when my palm rested a little too long on a pencil line and dragged it to the bottom of the page. I do my best to be meticulous with details, but sometimes, the drawing comes out a little blurry. I've always liked how the picture tells a story, and the manner I draw it does as well in the preciseness or aloofness of the features. Breaking my train of thought, Roland moans, his voice hoarse, full of emotion I can't figure out. I seriously doubt my pictures have moved him this much. When I look over, I see his face has turned redder.

"That's him!" He points accusingly at a portrait with a shaking finger. "That's Troy!" He turns to face me in astonishment. "How the hell do you have a drawing of Troy in your notebook?" He questions me in complete confusion.

We may be standing only a foot apart, but we might as well be on different continents. The distance between us expands as his suspicions grow. He gives me a once over, tearing at me with his mistrustful glare as though the answers are written on my forehead.

Hurt and confused, I move in closer to see what's gotten him so spooked. I have no idea what he's talking about. I've never met Troy before in my entire life.

With shaking hands, I pick up the book to take a closer look. Roland is as still as a statue as I study the unfamiliar image.

It's an old drawing, one I haven't looked at in years. It's situated at the beginning of the sketch book, one of my earliest charcoal portraits. The edges are faded, smudged by years of the pages rubbing against each other. The person isn't facing me directly. He is turned slightly, which is presumably how I'd seen him at the time.

Some of the features weren't well defined, as though I ran out of time while drawing or struggled to capture the details. The person's face is turned so only the profile is visible, but, there is one stark, shocking detail that is unmistakably present—a scar on the back of the head. Captured in charcoal, I'd highlighted it by leaving the area white to contrast it against the dark pencil marks.

I've never paid much attention to this drawing as I often draw people passing by or from my dreams. Yet there is something dark and haunting about this picture that I've never noticed before. I look closely, and I notice the way the man's shoulders slump, the heaviness of the jacket he's wearing, the set of his jaw.

Roland is right. In my hands is a portrait of Troy. In my sketch book. It's indisputable. This is him, the guy who assaulted Roland's sister, and the one who is now after me. How I came to draw him all those years ago, I have no idea.

CHAPTER 22

We both stare at the drawing in my hands equally at a loss for words. *What the hell? Have I met Troy before? If so, how? When?*

I sit heavily on the bed and close my eyes. The room spins and I gently lay the sketch book over my trembling knees, willing my heartbeat to slow down. Racking my brain, I search my memories to recall when I would have drawn a picture of Troy.

Taking a chance, I open my eyes and quickly glance at the bottom of the page. Scribbled there is the date when I made the drawing. According to this, I drew Troy over five years ago. No wonder I didn't recognize him. It must have been from a dream, but how would I even dream of someone I've never met?

He looks so different now, just like Roland has been saying all night. Still, no memories come to mind as to why I would have a portrait of him. I had just started to draw, so why would I feel compelled to create a piece based on someone I didn't know?

Roland reaches out and takes the book from my lap, leaving the empty space on my legs cold in its wake. Like a piece of my soul has left my body. I hold my breath as he begins to flip the pages in the sketch book, one by one, scrutinizing every detail, desperate to find any other clues in the pictures, perhaps even a second drawing of Troy. With every page turn, his shoulders dip slightly, his search coming up empty. Frustration builds around him like a crater forming beneath our feet. I feel like I'm sinking into the mattress, getting smaller, shrinking away, wanting to disappear.

I can tell he's using all the restraint he's got to not tear the pages right out of the book. His fingers are twitching, and he's working hard not to crumple up the drawing in his fist. He wants to respect me and my art, but he's struggling. His movements are sharp and fuming, yet he somehow manages to carefully turn the pages without ripping them. Is he angry with himself for blindly trusting me, a complete stranger? Or is it that I have a drawing of the man he despises the most in the world and can't explain it? I have a lot to answer for. Only, I have no clue where to begin. I still don't understand how I could possibly have a drawing of Troy in my sketchbook.

Sitting in front of him, I'm viewing the book upside down. All the portraits appear odd and skewed, but I easily recognize them. Since most of these were done more recently and took several hours to complete, I have vivid memories of completing them. I can typically decipher the images fairly easily from any angle. Some of the drawings are of classmates throughout the years; people captured at the local fair enjoying a hotdog; an old man laughing with his grandson on his knee in a park; a woman wrapping her shoulders with a blanket beside a bonfire.

I can still picture myself sprawled on my bed at my parents' house in Cornwall, up well into the early hours of the morning. My hand was cramped slightly from holding my pencil, my palm smudged black from running my hand over the piece.

I had been correcting lines with a round eraser, blowing pencil shavings off the crisp white page, letting them fall around me like saw dust, an artist's glitter. I could almost make out my shape in the midst of the mess as it surrounded me, the amount growing with each passing hour, before eventually, at the final stages, I'd declare the piece done—a masterpiece—and sign the bottom with my artist initials as well as adding the date below each.

Flipping through each page, Roland finally lands on my most recent drawing—the mystery woman. I hold my breath, waiting for comments to jab at me, his face contorted in a mixture of confusion and curiosity, but most of all, anger.

Inspecting her closely from this angle, I can't help but feel like she's alive and moving on the page. Her features are so crisp and fresh, not yet smudged like all the others. It's very clear that when I drew her, she was real in my mind, as though she'd been standing in front of me, modeling for me while I drew her. Yet, that hadn't been the case. I'd never seen her in real life, only in my head. But who's to say that wasn't real?

Flipping through the book, Roland finds my drawing of Troy again. What if I'd seen Troy in my mind as well? Had I really imagined him? Or was his image conjured from a long-ago forgotten memory? All those years ago, I'd drawn an image that I had no recollection about, an undefined picture with blurry lines that could have represented almost any guy who had crossed my path over the years. All identifying features were generic and abstract all except for one. How many people have a scar in the exact same location as Troy does?

And what if his portrait had been crisp and clear like this one? What if his had once been super defined, only to become warped and smudged over the years from the page rubbing on the others? Maybe the image had once been more defined, but I highly doubted that. I take great care of my sketch book, and I've been very careful about doing what I can to prevent the pages rubbing with others.

His image has more likely always been vague with smoothed edges—there but never really there. Not real, but real. A ghost of some sort, haunting me. A ghost only I could see. Only now, Roland has seen him too, had given him an identity and a name.

The name made him real. A threat.

Giving him a name had brought him back to life. A man who'd been hiding in the shadows for years, now back to cause mayhem in the lives of others.

But what does he want with me? Why did I draw him all those years ago? It's time to get answers. It's time to get out of here while there's still time.

CHAPTER 23

I scramble off the bed, suddenly alert. The hairs on the back of my neck stand up. I can hear my laboured breath echoing loudly in my own ears. I feel weak and tired, but I'm also acutely aware that something is wrong. Roland seems to notice the change also. We've only been in the room for a few moments, but we've been cut off from the rest of the manor, almost like we were somewhere else entirely, in our own bubble. We'd let our guards down, forgotten where we were. For a few minutes, there had been only Roland and me. Just us and my sketchbook full of unnamed faces.

Roland looks behind him and slowly begins to turn around. His movements are careful—calculated—as though some primal instinct is telling him not to make a sound. I just can't figure out if we need to stay silent so as not to alert someone to our whereabouts, or if we need to focus all of our attention on listening. Holding my breath, doing my part to void the room of noise, I strain my ears.

I don't hear anything. Nothing at all. I begin to relax and breathe normally only to have worry overtake me again. I don't hear anything. No sound whatsoever. My body convulses with fear as realization overwhelms my senses.

It's too quiet.

Where are all the others? I wonder. *How come they're suddenly so quiet?*

There are at least seven of us left. Surely at least one person would be moving or making noise of some sort. A sniffle, a shuffling of feet, the soft sound of fabric shifting along with body movements. As hard as I try, I can't make out any noise at all. I had half expected Troy to have vacated the premises as soon as he had the opportunity. Why stick around? He has a key after all. He's not locked in this prison like we are.

The lights flicker slightly; the storm only adding to the creepiness of the place. Roland eyes me warily, making it clear that he doesn't fully trust me anymore. He's probably debating heading out on his own. I'm not sure if he believes I am who I say I am anymore. I can't say I blame him. I'd be cautious too if the roles were reversed. But what can he possibly think I've done? How has he made any sense of this in his mind? I'd love to be enlightened. Maybe it would explain all of this. But there's no time to sit and chat. Something is off.

Taking a quick breath, I hesitantly step towards the doorframe. Peering out, I find the hallway empty. Where the hell is everyone?

Turning back towards Roland, I see him still clutching my sketchbook. A single tear slips down his cheek as he stares at the drawing of Troy. I can only imagine the emotions Roland must be feeling right now, seeing an image of Reese's attacker as he'd looked when he'd hurt her.

Hesitating, wanting to be respectful, yet feeling a sense of dread overtaking me, I walk over to him and gently place my hand on his forearm to get his attention.

"Roland, you have to believe me. I have no idea why this drawing is in here. I promise you I have no memory of ever meeting Troy. I don't remember drawing this." He's listening, but he still doesn't know what to believe. I press on, "I mean, look at the date. Isn't this around the same year Troy hurt Reese? How could I have run into him at that time? Wouldn't he have been in jail already?" Pointing to the bottom of the page to prove my point, I add, "I can't explain how his portrait ended up in my sketchbook, but we really need to focus right now."

He turns to face me, his cheeks stained with wet streaks from his tears. Some droplets land on the sketch of Troy, but I don't care. None of it matters anymore.

A man who was a stranger to me only hours before is crying before me, and I feel a tug in my heart. I pull him close for a hug, and he collapses into my arms, finally letting go. I stroke his hair gently, doing my best to soothe the pain he holds tightly inside. My lips are near his ear, but I remain quiet. I want to whisper something supportive to help ease the hurt, but I can't. I have no idea what to say that could possibly make any of this better.

Holding on to him, I'm relieved that Roland seems to have let down his guard, at least for the time being. He might have been suspicious of me, my role in this entire thing as blurry as Troy's drawing, but whatever caused me to draw the picture in the first place had nothing to do with this moment right now. Roland needs me, and I'm more than happy to be there for him.

I don't know how long we stand there, arms interlocked, not moving or swaying, but holding on firmly to each other as though our bodies are holding each other up. But I don't dare move.

Eventually, he pulls away from me, slowly and somewhat reluctantly. Our faces are inches from each other, and I spot flecks of gold in his eyes. He removes his glasses and rubs at his eyes, the rims of them slightly red. His thick lashes are still wet from his tears, and his cheeks have a beautiful peach tone to them. His nose has a dusting of freckles I hadn't noticed before.

My breathing increases as our stares seem to penetrate deep within our souls. Embarrassed and feeling too hot, I back away, removing my hands from his back. *How can I be doing this with another man?* I scold myself.

Thank God nothing happened. We'd almost kissed. I just knew it. And based on Roland's fidgety stance, he'd known it too. I would never forgive myself if I ever cheated on Xavier, yet the pull towards Roland is so strong it's practically magnetic.

I'll have to be much more careful from now on, to keep a safe distance from him at all times, to do my best to push against the force that keeps pulling us closer together. It's as though the universe wants us together like we're connected somehow.

Returning my attention to the room, I force myself to look at him while I speak, refusing to let him know how much his presence affects every cell in my body, how badly I want to touch him again. *No, don't go there*, I plead with myself. I can't believe this. I'm so weak.

Roland, look, I'm sorry, I can't. I have a boyfriend whom I love very much. There. How easy is that to say? Yet, I don't say it, out of pride or fear perhaps. And what if Roland doesn't feel anything between us? Then I'm just a girl blabbing on, being way too personal for no reason.

Instead, I busy myself by searching through my bag to retrieve my hoodie and pull it on. I haven't stopped shivering since we discovered Sadie's body growing cold in the stairwell. The shock of finding her mixed with the eeriness of the night, and the dropping temperature have caused my teeth to chatter.

I can tell Roland has noticed. He takes a small step towards me but stops, thinking better of it. To avoid any more tension, I turn my back to him so he won't see the embarrassment creep up my face.

"The hallway is strangely quiet, don't you think?" I say, obviously.

Clearing his throat, Roland agrees, "Definitely strange. We need to get out of here." He takes a glance around the room but can't seem to find what he's searching for.

"See if you can find anything sharp, or hard. Anything that could be used as a weapon," he whispers.

My eyes grow big as the words enter my mind.

"What? Why?" I stammer.

"If Troy is still here lurking around a corner, he might have hurt the others while we were in your room. He's already hurt and killed two people. What's stopping him from coming in here and attacking us?"

He spots a fire extinguisher beside the door, grabs it with one hand and brings a finger to his lips. He motions for me to follow him, and together, we leave the safety of Room Eight and head out into the dark, empty hallway.

CHAPTER 24

The darkness envelops us completely making me shiver in my sweatshirt. My head feels itchy from stress sweat and from the glue of the electrodes. It feels like so long ago when Sadie had fastened them to my skull. A small sob escapes my lips as I think about her now, dead and alone in the stairwell. I try not to think about the other woman Troy attacked down the hall. I didn't even know her name. I promise myself that if I make it out of here alive, I will learn her name.

Whatever Troy is doing, she hadn't been part of the plan—I just know it in my gut. She was an unfortunate casualty, in the wrong place at the wrong time. I don't believe for a second that her death was premeditated. Still, it doesn't change the atrocity of it, the absolute horror show that has become of this night.

Troy is after me. I can feel it in my bones. The reason why, I haven't figured out yet, but I feel it deep within that he's coming for me next.

I walk closely behind Roland as we make our way down the hall. Taking small, careful steps, we keep turning our heads to try and catch sight of something that will provide insight into our situation. There are no noises, the lights are off, and there are no vibrations to indicate other living beings scurrying around in here.

Darkly, the stillness reminds me of an old Christmas poem my mother would recite every year, entitled 'A Visit from St. Nicholas'. I can't help but think of the passage "not a creature was stirring, not even a mouse."

I see Roland's shoulders slump. He feels it too. We are alone. Somehow, the others have gone. Did they find a way out? Are they still alive? Why does the idea of being alone seem more ominous than having a killer after us?

Shaking the images from my mind before they completely consume me, I do my best to focus on the task before us. I can't bear the thought of more dead bodies. It's just too horrible to fathom.

Walking together at a steady pace, only the sounds of our soft footfalls on the velvet carpet and our shallow breaths can be heard now. Suddenly, Roland stops in his tracks, and I crash into his back, bumping my nose on it. I whimper, feeling hot tears in my eyes from the pain that shoots through me.

Without uttering a single word, Roland, still on the lookout, reaches behind him without bothering to turn around. He finds my hand and takes it in his stroking my hand with his thumb gently as though checking to see if I'm alright. His touch makes me melt in place, not like a witch who got a bucket of water dumped over her head, but rather like sweet chocolate that's melting over the soft glow of a candle waiting for berries to be dipped—delicious.

This small, unexpected act of kindness makes my insides warm up all at once, instantly thawing every last bit of coldness that had taken residence in my bones.

Without letting go of my hand, Roland escorts me down the hall. Together we make it to the exit, as we had before. Turning to me, he leans in close enough for me to be enveloped by his scent.

"We have to be extremely quiet. I'm not sure if Troy is still here or not, and I don't want to find out." I nod at this, feeling the same.

"I didn't check the exit door the last time because, well..." There was a dead body in the way. He doesn't say it, but I know what he means, so I nod. I feel sick.

The idea of having to walk over Sadie's body, of leaving her behind, to get out of here, while her body remains locked in this place, terrifies me. I fight the panic rising in my chest as my breathing and heartbeat begin to speed up.

"Look at me, Laurel," Roland utters calmly. "I'll keep you safe. Stay close to me and we'll be alright." Offering a slight smile, I almost believe it.

He's clutching onto the fire extinguisher with one hand and holding my hand with his other. We arrive at the exit door and stop walking. We know what's beyond this door, and neither of us are eager to push through.

I take a deep breath steadying myself, and feel Roland's hand tighten around mine, comforting me. *Together*, the gesture says. Whatever is beyond this door, we'll face it together.

Closing my eyes, doing my best to protect my mind from what I'm about to see, I hear Roland gasp beside me. His grip on my hand lessens as my eyes open to see nothing. Or rather, no one. Sadie's body is no longer lying on the ground where it had been only moments before. Someone has moved her. But why?

"What the hell?" I hear myself say in disbelief.

"What's going on here?" Roland echoes my feelings, dropping my hand. "Where is she?" Frantic, he begins to pace the tiny space, placing the fire extinguisher against the wall near the door. He folds himself over the railing to get a better look at the bottom of the stairs, but evidently finds nothing.

He scratches his head and lets out a nervous laugh. "I don't get it." Lifting his hands in surrender, he shakes his head. "I give up. I've got no idea what's going on here."

He looks over at me, but I don't offer any explanation. I'm just as lost as he is.

We're both exhausted, and our adrenaline is running out. This place is freaking me out. I just want to go home even though home has been just as strange these days. Right now, I'm not sure home is where I want to go, but it's better than this place. Anything is better than here.

I'm about to suggest finding a way out, when we hear a muffled noise coming from down below. We rush down the stairs two steps at a time and see a small, door right beside the stairs. It looks like a closet and there is a large lock on the door. Roland pulls at it, but it doesn't budge. We can hear shuffling inside and muffled voices. We look at each other, dread creeping around us as we finally understand where everyone went.

CHAPTER 25

We can hear subdued banging and screaming coming from somewhere down below us. The walls are all made of concrete making the yells seem muffled and distant. The door is made of ridiculously thick wood, stained with several coats of lacquer, fortifying it, making it practically impenetrable. Even the hinges look menacing made with intricate black iron with large spiky, square nails securing them in place leaving them completely unmoving.

"There must be some kind of cellar or basement through here," Roland guesses.

How Troy managed to single-handedly force all of these people into the basement baffles me. I try pushing on the door as hard as I can, but nothing happens.

"Laurel, get behind me," Roland urges before he gives the door a hard kick. His foot slams against the door, and he stumbles backwards from the force of it. Still, nothing happens. It doesn't even budge.

"These old estates were built like fortresses. We won't be able to break through this door," he sighs, exhausted and seemingly defeated.

But I refuse to give up. I suddenly remember that we came to this stairwell armed with something. I break into a run, back up the stairs and grab hold of the fire extinguisher.

Rushing back down the stairs, I trip, barely catching the wooden banister before face-planting at Roland's feet, dropping the fire extinguisher on the ground. I must still be a little wobbly from finding Sadie's body earlier, and from not sleeping tonight.

"Are you okay?" His eyes are filled with worry as he helps me up. I nod, more embarrassed than hurt.

The loud banging seems to escalate, and more fists have joined in. They know we're here, just on the other side of this door. Their desperation can be heard in the screams and restless pounding. They're talking to us, but we can't figure out the words. The thickness of the door prevents the words from reaching us, only allowing sounds through. It seems useless standing here not being able to reach them. They're right on the other side of this door, but they might as well be in a different building.

Grabbing the fire extinguisher at my feet, I hand it to Roland and he swings it hard against the door. Similar to before, nothing happens. If anything, the red canister is slightly dented now, but the door remains untouched, the lathered-on veneer protecting the surface, rendering it glossy and slippery. Like a thick shell, protecting whatever is behind that door. It makes me think of photos I've seen of the ice storm of 1998, when every surface was covered with inch-thick ice strong enough to bend trees and break fences. Giving up on the fire extinguisher, he abandons it on the floor. Peering at the door more closely, I scratch at its surface with my nail. What is this stuff? Anything we try to hit on it will simply slide right off, diminishing the force of the impact.

"Maybe there's something we can use to break this lock somewhere in this place." I suggest finally, trying a new tactic. "Maybe we can find a tool in a storage room? Or perhaps another patient has something in their room we could use as a weapon?"

Roland shrugs his shoulders and wipes beads of sweat from his forehead. "Worth a shot." His breath is winded.

"Alright, you stay here and keep trying to break down the door, and I'll go back and check the rooms," I offer, sounding braver than I feel.

I think my plan will work. Surely I'll find something useful against this lock, but Roland shakes his head, adamantly rejecting my suggestion.

"No," he says, lifting a hand and, stopping me in my tracks. His tone is decisive. "We need to stick together." He takes a step towards me. "I don't trust that psycho around you. Together we stand a chance, but if you go alone, I don't want to think about what could happen." I see a shudder course through his body.

"Okay. Together, then," I nod, feeling relieved that I won't have to go exploring the darkness on my own.

CHAPTER 26

We walk back up the stairs in silence quietly contemplating our situation. None of this makes any sense. Why would Troy lock everyone up? We already know he's not afraid of hurting others, or even killing. So why bother entrapping everyone, witnesses who will get out eventually and spill his secrets? It makes no sense and it doesn't seem to fit.

Opening the stairwell door, we find ourselves back in the hallway, and Roland's hand instinctively clasps mine. He's so protective of me, but in a good way. I can tell he's not trying to hold me back, but rather to provide reassurance with his presence. For a fleeting moment, I allow myself to imagine us as a couple, casually taking a stroll through town, out buying expensive coffees before finding a quiet patio for lunch. I can visualize it—us together.

The thought warms me at first, but then takes me aback. I'm surprised at how easily I can forget about Xavier, my boyfriend of over two years. When did I become the sort of girlfriend who emotionally cheats on her guy? That's not me. I should pull my hand away. I should tell him that I'm taken. But I don't. His hand is warm, and I'm terrified.

Surely Xavier would understand my predicament. I'm fearing for my life right now. My warm feelings and inclination towards this other man might be excused or explained as survival instinct.

Maybe Xavier will even thank Roland at the end of all of this for taking such good care of me, and for seeing that I came out of it safely. If I weren't shaking so badly, I'd probably chuckle at how ridiculous I sound, even to myself. Xavier would never be okay with this even though Roland's actions, so far, have only been to comfort and reassure me that I'm not alone. I look over at Roland. I know he's got my back and that we'll fight this together.

With a sinking feeling I realize that Xavier has never made me feel like we were a team; like it was us against the world. He's always tried to one-up me, always tried to appear superior, in charge of his life and of mine. He didn't appreciate my outburst the other night because it had made him afraid. I had threatened his masculinity by accidently punching him. And instead of forgiving me and trying to understand what was going on with me, he'd lashed out. It was his way of regaining control of the situation. Never allowing himself to be the weak one, he needed to remind me that I was smaller and weaker than him.

Was that really the kind of relationship I wanted for myself? For my boyfriend to constantly belittle me, to push me down when I'm getting too high up so that he doesn't lose his precious place in the spotlight of our relationship?

Suddenly it was like I could see Xavier under the spotlight and just like that, it became so clear to me.

I'd always been scared to lose him, this great, larger-than-life man. I'd mistakenly assumed that being under his umbrella and, getting his attention was love. How wrong I'd been. Xavier didn't love me for who I was. At the very first sign of a flaw, he'd balked and freaked out on me. He'd tried to contain me and placed me in a corner, like some untamed animal.

It was the first time I'd understood. Xavier loved the idea of me—a pretty, artsy girlfriend—but the minute I'd truly struggle, he would disappear. He couldn't handle his perfect girlfriend to be flawed. How did I go along with it for so long? How did I not notice this before? I guess, until now, I'd never had anyone to compare to. I'd been spellbound, thinking he was everything I ever wanted.

I'd only ever been in one serious relationship in my entire life—with Xavier. How was I to know that our relationship wasn't healthy? On the surface, Xavier seems so kind, funny, and handsome, but in reality, he's controlling and manipulative. He'd basically been grooming me for the last few years to be the girlfriend he thought would be worthy of being with him.

I finally understand what my mom's been trying to warn me about. I'd been so blinded by love, or what I thought was love, that I'd ignored her pleas to see Xavier for who he really was.

She's never liked him.

Her guard had gone up the very first time they'd met. She'd smiled at him, fooling him perhaps, but I'd easily recognized my mother's smile. Her lips had stretched across her mouth in a tight line, never quite reaching her eyes. But that smile had been fake, for his benefit alone, effectively feigning politeness all the while rejecting my choice in a partner.

I remember how mad I'd been with her once I confronted her about it. To my astonishment, she hadn't even tried to skirt around the issue. She hadn't even had the decency to lie for my sake. Instead, she'd been direct and very harsh about her feelings towards him.

She didn't think he was good for me, but when pressed, wouldn't say why. I guess in some ways, she was trying to protect me, but at the time it only left me shattered. Her abrupt and unshakable dismissal of my choices tore our mother-daughter bond, permanently severing it to where it rests now, always guarded, stepping on eggshells. I've never been able to let myself speak fully and honestly around her since.

I should have listened to her. Shaking my head, the weight of regret on my shoulders, I can't believe I ever let a guy break what I had with my mother. She was my best friend, always had been. I should have heard her out, at the very least. I should have known that she had my best interests in mind. She'd always put my own happiness before hers, sacrificing her own feelings. How foolish I'd been to ever doubt her intentions.

I'll need to fix things up with her whenever we get out of here—if we ever do. I can't die in this strange place. I won't. At least, not before I get the chance to patch things up with her.

Breaking my train of thought, Roland stops walking.

"You know, I bet that other technologist would have had keys for the basement door. She would at least have keys to unlock one of the exterior doors so we could go get help. We just need to find out where Troy put her."

He's right. It's a good plan, but where do we even begin looking? What if Sadie is stuck in that basement along with everyone else? Then what?

CHAPTER 27

One room at a time, we search together. Sometimes I'm on the lookout while he's searching through belongings. Other times we switch. So far, there have been no signs of Troy. Maybe he's left the building altogether. Yet, something tells me he's still here. There's a ringing energy—evil, all around us. I'm convinced he's still here. But where? Why? And what is he doing?

"Look at this!" Roland exclaims, lifting the old man's cane from Room Seven. "I bet I could do some serious damage with this if I swung it at his head." He lifts it with both arms as though it were a baseball bat and I wince. "Or even break some bones, just to slow him down," he suggests, but his face falls. "I hate that guy, Laurel. I do. He's the scum of the earth and he destroyed my sister's life. But I don't know if I've got it in me to actually hurt him." He sinks on the bed clutching the cane in his hands, twisting it around.

"I get it. I hope it won't come to that, but Troy is a ticking timebomb right now. He's already killed two people in one night. Who knows what else he's planning?" I say and immediately feel dread race through my veins.

It's almost as though I've just jinxed us, tempted fate and egged on the evil spirit Troy has looming over him. Roland grimaces slightly, probably wishing I'd kept my mouth shut.

"Hey, look at this." He rubs a finger over a button on the cane.

He presses it and we both jump up, fully alert. "Wow!" he says, his mouth agape, clearly surprised. "I wasn't expecting that!"

The button has released a sharp, metallic prong-like piece at the bottom of the cane. The sharp spike winks at us in the low light. Its usual purpose is to help people walk on icy roads and sidewalks, but it might become very useful if we need to defend ourselves.

"Now, this could work." Grinning, he looks up, an expression of bewilderment on his face as though he can't believe what we're doing. Two strangers looking for weapons while trying to locate missing people, hunt down a killer, and escape this fortress-like manor.

"Okay, this is good. At least we have something! Let's keep looking," I prompt him, pushing away my unease, compartmentalizing the idea of ever needing to use this on Troy.

Eagerly and efficiently, we move from room to room, scavenging random items that might be useful. In Chris's room, we find a leather belt and a framed picture of a baby girl.

The baby couldn't have been older than six months. A cute, pink onesie with stars covers her toes and fits snuggly around an adorable Buddha-belly. She has a beautiful flower headband and tiny fluffs of hair covering her head. At the time the picture was taken, it's clear that she'd just recently learned how to sit on her own without assistance so someone had taken the extra precaution of strategically placing a giant stuffed bear behind her and soft blankets all around her in case she fell before they got to her.

So maybe Chris had been drinking all that coffee because he was a new dad. I can almost picture him standing just out of the shot, anxious and at the ready should his daughter begin to show any signs of falling; prepared to catch her. I hadn't pictured him as a dad, but then again, I hardly knew any of these people at all.

Going through everyone's belongings had made me uncomfortable at first, but the longer we search the more concerned I'm beginning to feel.

The halls are still eerily quiet, but we know for certain that Troy is lurking around. From the way he's working, quickly and quietly, it's almost like he's playing a game with us, a game we have no desire to play.

I sigh as I rifle through man-bun guy's duffle bag, wrinkling my nose when my hand lands on dirty boxer shorts. Gross. I try not to let my disdain show too much. We have bigger things to worry about than skid marks and pubic hair stuck to dirty underwear. I cringe, making a mental note to wash my hands thoroughly afterwards, assuming I'll have the time to do so.

As I carefully inspect the rest of the bag, Roland lets out a soft exclamation coming over to me to show me his find.

"Are you kidding me? That's gold!" I say excitedly, staring at the small Swiss army knife.

"I found it in his shoe!" he exclaims.

Jackpot, I think.

It's small but mighty, easy to conceal, yet capable of doing real harm. We try out the various features, giddy with our find. The small, jewel-like weapon has a glossy red coating with over thirty functions. Flipping each one open carefully, we find several sharp blades, a corkscrew, scissors, a saw, some metal files, screwdrivers, pliers, a stainless-steel pin, wire cutters and a can opener.

"Okay, let's keep searching," I prompt. I have no concept of the time, but I know we're running short of it.

Walking down the hall towards the middle-aged woman's room, Roland stops short.

"Hey." He brandishes the Swiss-army knife. "I might be able to use some of these tools on the basement door hinges to pop it open. It's a long shot. Those hinges looked practically welded on, but maybe..." He appears hopeful.

"If you think so," I say, trying to keep the skeptical tone out of my voice.

"I'll go try it now, if that's okay with you?" He starts for the exit and stops. "I think I should go alone, just in case Troy is lurking around there. We don't know if this will work. I don't want both of us to end up in his trap if he is planning something."

Pausing, he steps out into the hallway to retrieve an item from our meager stack of acquired weapons. Grabbing the cane and thrusting it in my hands, he instructs. "Take this and hide in the closest room. Don't open the door for anyone except for me. Okay?" His eyes search mine, waiting for my small nod before he sprints away.

I look after him, willing him to come back for me. I don't want to be left alone, but mostly, I don't want him to go.

The fear I'd been pushing away begins to cover my body feeling like tiny ants crawling all over my skin as I watch him disappear through the doors. I feel completely powerless. I'm alone in the hallway, suddenly aware of how vulnerable I am. I could wait here in this very spot until Roland returns, but I know it would be a waste of time. I swallow down my nervousness, do as I'm told, and step into the other woman's dark room.

The sight is too horrible to look at directly. Shutting my eyes and holding my breath, afraid to breathe in anything unpleasant, I crash hard against the wall, but it's too late—I've already seen it.

I feel my breathing intensifying. My heartbeat rattles in my chest as the room spins in circles around me. I haven't experienced this sensation often, but there isn't a single doubt in my mind that I'm about to have a panic attack.

Leaning on the wall, realizing it's the only thing holding me up right now, I let myself slide down the cool surface until my body collides hard with the floor. Feeling the soreness of the impact, I'm sure I'll be left with a massive bruise, and I'll struggle to sit for a few days. Yet, none of that matters to me right now.

When I force my eyes open, my vision is spotty. I focus on my breathing. My throat is hoarse. Blinking steadily until my eyes unwillingly adjust to the dark, I whimper. Even from her silhouette I can tell she's dead. The way she's lying is unnatural. Her arms are tied behind her back securing her body to a chair. Her head is snapped backwards, too far. Her neck has been slashed and blood has poured out, pooling under the chair.

Pushing myself up from the floor, I step closer. Stifling a sob in my throat, I will myself to check her wrist for a pulse. I must just in case. Unsurprisingly, and somewhat gratefully, there is none. I'm surprised to be relieved to discover that she's dead. At least her suffering didn't drag on for too long.

Looking over her body, I finally realize that she's naked from the waist down. Her pants and underwear have been pulled down and rest, crumpled at her ankles. There is a bloody handprint on one of her thighs, and I almost gag. I quickly turn away, out of respect or out of sickness; maybe both.

This poor woman! She came to Salter Square to get help for a sleep disorder, only to be attacked, humiliated, and murdered. It is absolutely despicable. And for what? Because she's a woman Troy believes he has the right to tear her apart? I feel sick, thinking of Troy's hands running over her body and torturing her while we were all otherwise occupied. And for what purpose other than to fulfill his sexual arousal, to satiate his hatred for women?

Intense revulsion builds up inside of me, and I have the sudden desire to break things.

I stare at this woman's lifeless form and fight the urge to move her to a more dignified position. This woman had a life. She might have had a family, people who will be grieving for her, missing her. Perhaps she has daughters who will grow up without their mother. Who will they turn to when they want to talk about boys, or their period, or how to dress for prom? Her husband will be a widower. How long until he finds love again? And what if she has sons? Would they ever be able to heal from this? Or would they seek revenge? The thoughts blur together as the tears run down my face.

I can't do this.

I must not allow myself to think this way. I don't know if she had kids or a husband. Maybe she did, maybe not. Either way, what happened to her is inexcusable and horrible, yet I can't let these sad, terrible thoughts take over. If I do, they will cripple me—paralyze me in place.

I have to focus.

There are still the others and Roland. I can't save this woman—that much is clear. Why hide everyone else but leave her here out in the open in this horrible state for us to find?

Abruptly, it's very clear to me. I begin to step away from the body, my hands open and rigid at my sides. I'm terrified to touch anything else. It's obvious what's going on. This woman has been left on display—perfectly positioned—to be seen. This is all a show.

Troy must have left her here as a message to anyone who dared cross his path. To demonstrate what he's capable of, and to let us know what he plans to do if he gets to us. I recoil thinking of how narrowly I avoided a similar sad fate when he'd been in my room earlier. I'd been in deep sleep and completely vulnerable. If it hadn't been for Sadie's intervention, who knows what would have become of me?

My shoulders tremble as I begin to back out of the cramped space. Suddenly there doesn't seem to be enough air in here.

"There you are."

A voice comes from behind me and I freeze, too scared to turn around. I drop the cane.

CHAPTER 28

My back tenses as I turn my head slowly.

"Oh my God, Roland! You scared the crap out of me!" I grimace at him, hitting him in the chest semi-playfully, but mostly angrily. "I thought you were Troy!" I exhale and surprise myself by starting to cry uncontrollably. "You can't sneak up on me like that! Okay? It's creepy!"

"Hey, hey," he shushes me gently. "It's okay. It's just me. You're okay," he says, pulling me into a hug.

He holds me tightly in his arms, caressing my hair and comforting me, and I feel myself coming back as I release waterfalls of tears, soaking the front of his shirt. He doesn't seem to mind too much. He appears more concerned about me than about his clothes, but I still feel bad for leaving streaks of wet tears on his clothes.

"Sorry. It's just too much. All of this." I wave a hand behind me so he can see the body in the room.

Stepping aside, I watch him take it in.

He swallows a hard lump in his throat, and I see him force it down as a sob bubbles up to escape from between his lips. Just like I did, he steps forward, tentatively, but I reach out my hand to stop him. I'll save him the trouble. He looks back and I shake my head almost unnoticeably. *She's gone*, it says.

I see despair etched over his face and he turns around again to face the brutal scene. His hands fly to his face as he struggles to keep it together. Only moments ago, it had been me who'd been in shock. Roland had been comforting me, but now the roles have reversed. There's nothing I can do but wait for him to go through the range of feelings. As the shock wears off, I see him close his eyes and shake his head, trying to erase the image from his mind, but like for me, it will be burnt there forever. After a moment, he clenches his jaw and forms fists with his hands. Finally, he's feeling what I need him to feel.

Anger.

I see it radiating off of him, like a halo of fire, and I'm right there with him. I'm scared. I'm tired. But most of all, I'm fucking pissed off.

"Roland, look. I'm mad too, okay? This asshole needs to be stopped. What he did to this woman is pure evil."

Avoiding another look in her direction, I focus my eyes on Roland's. They are filled with tears and red from tiredness and anger.

"I'm going to kill him!" he roars and rushes past me into the hallway.

Oh no, this isn't good, I begin to worry. "Wait, Roland! You're not thinking clearly! Please, stop!" I plead as I pick up the cane and chase after him.

In the hallway, I find him a few feet away, bent over our stack of weapons lying in the middle of the hall. Taking in the scene, I remain quiet and gently drop the cane on top of the pile before helping him sift through the items to select the ones we'll use against Troy.

"Now we know he has a knife...and that he's not afraid to use it." Roland barely looks at me, his focus on finding a suitable weapon. "He's diverted from his pattern."

"What do you mean?"

"My sister—she's petite, with long hair and, blue eyes, in her mid-twenties. That woman in there was closer to fifty, with short hair, brown eyes, and a heavier build. That's not Troy's normal pattern. Something's changed." He looks away pensively for a moment.

"His pattern? You mean, there were others?" My voice comes out as a squeak. I don't mean to sound scared, but my voice betrays me.

Roland exhales and hangs his head. "Yes. Troy admitted that much, but those girls have never come forward. I wonder if he threatened them or something. Or maybe they just don't know."

"How could they not know?" I ask bewildered, but then I remember how Troy had used my night terrors to sneak into my room unnoticed. He was clever and patient. A true predator. I jolt at the thought.

"Look, I'm not trying to scare you, but Troy is dangerous. He's armed and, well, now for whatever reason, he's also extremely unpredictable. Picture a wild animal baring teeth, with froth coming out of its mouth." The image is clearly imprinted in my brain. "We know what he's capable of. We need to arm ourselves in case we bump into him. Better to be prepared."

I simply nod in reply.

He's right. It doesn't matter that I've never used a weapon in my life. I'll need one anyway. If I run into Troy, it will be my best chance against him. There will be no reasoning with him in this state. We know who he is, and he knows that. He's cornered like a trapped animal—desperate. Even if he runs, we know the truth. If we can just get out of this place, we can report all of this to the police and they can search for him.

Our search only yields a few useful things, and for most of them we have to keep an open mind and use our creativity to figure out how they could be useful against a dangerous person like Troy. I look at our pathetic pile and feel the adrenaline I'd had earlier drain out of me. Suddenly, I just want to go to bed and sleep forever.

Amongst the items is a shoelace that we could use to tie his hands with or strangle him. I also have the geometry set I brought with me. I was hoping to use the sharp triangular ruler to stab Troy, but Roland had quickly vetoed this idea, pointing out that I would cut my hand way worse than any wound I'd inflict on Troy.

Other items were scavenged from the men's rooms; spray cologne to squirt into his eyes and momentarily blind him; a large book to hit him with, and hopefully knock him out. From Roland's room, we grabbed his plastic toothbrush, which he broke in half and held up for a quick inspection so that I could see the surprisingly sharp end of it. It wasn't much, but at least we weren't going to be meeting Troy completely empty-handed.

After only seconds of deliberation, Roland pockets the Swiss-army knife and grabs the old man's cane. Without pausing, he stands abruptly and begins haphazardly checking in each and every room, quickly jogging between each one of them until we reach the control room.

I hurry behind him, wrapping the shoelace around my wrist and gripping tightly onto the severed toothbrush.

I fall in step behind him as he enters the control room, his attention pulled by something in front of him. Once inside the small room, I'm overwhelmed by all the lit-up monitors, dozens of grey screens staring back at us. I wasn't too keen on the idea of being filmed as I slept, but maybe there's something here that can help us. Perhaps we can even find out where Sadie is and find the keys to get out and get help.

Transfixed by the grainy, low-quality monitors observing us like a fly's eye, I feel very exposed, even though no cameras seem to be present in this room. Roland attempts to open a browser to access the internet, but after several seconds, it's clear that the computers aren't connected to an external server.

Cramped in this small space, I begin to feel hot all over. As if I'm having a hot-flash, I feel like my body temperature has rapidly sky-rocketed and I fight the urge to remove my sweater. The sudden wall of heat must be from all the monitors in the room and the lack of ventilation. Thankfully we've left the door ajar, because otherwise I'd most likely be having a full-blown panic attack right now.

I'm about the turn around and step back out in the hall when Roland gets my attention. While I was mainly trying to breathe and keep from passing out, he'd been exploring the small space, looking for clues. How he manages to keep cool under this amount of pressure is astounding. I wish I were able to be this calm and collected, but I'm a hot mess. I'm not proud of it—it just is what it is.

Holding up a manila folder, he points to the name on the tab: Laurel Gervais.

I'm not entirely surprised to see this as I was referred to the sleep clinic by my doctor. But seeing a file with my name on it in Roland's hands gives me a jolt. The desk is littered with stacks of folders. I debate searching through them to find out the name of the older woman in order to remember her properly, to respect her in memory, but my feet are stuck in place. I can't move from my position.

Next to me, Roland is seething. He's gripping my file tightly, denting the thick paper's surface. I know I'm slower than usual at reaching conclusions tonight. It's driving me insane. Typically, my imagination runs wild, but tonight, I can only focus on what's in front of me—not seeing the entire staircase, only the first step. It's taking everything for me to snap out of this trance I seem to be in. I barely recognize myself. I'm usually the first one to see the big picture, to suggest alternatives, to be one step ahead. This new sensation makes me uncomfortable. I can't help but feel useless.

My hands begin to itch; it's a tic I get when I feel anxious. Normally, I would ease the tension in my body by sketching something, to release some pressure and change my focus from emotion to something more concrete, something more easily manipulated. I would try to take control of the feelings, but tonight I can't. I don't see far enough. I can't reach where Roland already is in his thoughts. I'm only focused on this moment, the here and now. On surviving the next few minutes.

I'm about to ask Roland what the big deal is with the folders, when he slams the file down on the desk next to him.

Pressing his palms against the edge of the desk, to steady himself, his head down and, eyes closed, he sighs, "Troy had access to all of this information."

Realization settles in around me like little droplets of icy rain, each stinging me in small slivers, increasing with each passing second. Opening the file once again, Roland begins to pull out sheets of paper and read off of them. " 'Laurel Gervais, aged 20, student at Carter College in Graphic Design.' It has your address and your doctor's information, too. Your blood type, your previous medical history, information about past night terrors. It's all here." He sighs. "All in one neat little package. A gift in the wrong hands."

Looking through the files, I find a woman's name. The only other female patient here tonight, the one from Room Five. Her name was Madeline Cloutier. I pause, taking this in, letting her name make an imprint on my brain. Flipping the folder, I scan the pages and falter. Madeline Cloutier was married to a Rich Cloutier, and they have two young sons, ages five and seven. Biting my bottom lip to keep from weeping, I carefully close the file, hug it to my chest as a makeshift goodbye, and place it back on the desk.

I watch Roland pull out another file, this time with his name on it. After flipping through a few pages, he looks up at me, worry etched across his face.

"Laurel, this is bad. Even if we can find a way to escape this place, Troy knows exactly who we are and where to find us."

Not knowing what to say, I simply stare back. In a way, I'm hoping that all of this has been a dream; that I'll be waking up any moment now, getting out of Salter Square, and cramming last minute notes before my exam. Unfortunately, this is all too real. How many times do we confuse our dreams with reality, when in fact, it's our reality we should be scared of?

CHAPTER 29

Roland rubs his forehead trying to come up with a plan, maybe thinking of where to go, what to do. I feel useless, stuck in this very spot, my mind numb and slushy. There's a persistent throbbing behind my eyes, so I close my eyelids momentarily hoping for a reprieve, but it doesn't stop the annoying flashes of light. I need sleep. I'm stressed, I'm exhausted, and most of all, I'm afraid.

Opening my eyes, my attention lands on the empty coffee mug with a residue of pink lipstick smeared over the rim. A sob escapes my throat as I think of Sadie. In her last moments she was trying to protect me from a vicious attacker, only to place herself right in his path. I won't ever get the opportunity to thank her for her bravery, for her actions, for her sacrifice. I won't ever get to tell her how sorry I am that she suffered because of me. Because I unwillingly started this entire thing. It's all my fault, somehow.

Troy came to find me. He was inside my room. To do what? I'm still not sure, but based on what Roland told me earlier about his sister and from seeing the two battered women tonight, it's pretty clear to me that his intentions were anything but good. All hope is lost for this man.

He's gone too far to the dark side. Salter Square must have been a playground for him, a creepy prison with vulnerable victims where he's the ruler who knows all the secret passages. Where he gets to watch without being seen, to observe from the shadows with demons decorating the walls.

Under the cover of night, Troy feels safe. He's at home here, in this manor. This place is fitting for him. It provides opportunities—places to hide himself and to hide people. A place where things disappear, and people die.

How close had Troy been to getting what he'd come for? How long had he been standing in my room, quietly observing me, without me having the slightest idea? He could easily have watched me sleep from his seat in the control room, but for some reason, he'd wanted more. He'd needed to be closer, close enough to touch, to smell, and to hurt.

The idea that we breathed in the same air for any amount of time, repulses me.

He'd been so close, yet I hadn't noticed him. I'd been completely unguarded, covered with a false sense of security, hiding beneath the blankets like a child with a nightmare. Only the monster wasn't under the bed or in the closet. He'd been at my feet, pulling, reaching, clawing at my skin. I'd fought back, my unconscious mind aware enough to protect me in the best way it could, but he'd had the advantage.

The vivid images from the night terror are pixelated, distorted. I can't put them back together into something tangible. I can't order them back. It's like my mind is protecting me from the memories. They are filed away, locked up. What kind of secrets would my mind reveal if it were suddenly unlocked?

Fragments of images, remembrance of feelings. That's all I'm able to muster from tonight's episode. Normally, I'd be relieved not to remember the night terror—too horrible to ever revisit—trusting my mind to know what's best for me. But now, at this moment, I'd do just about anything to regain those memories, to peek behind the curtain of my subconscious. The answers are right there inside of my mind but inaccessible. I could just scream.

Exhaling loudly, I release the built-up tension as best as I can and bite the inside of my cheek, hard. I taste blood. Licking my wound, I try to bring myself back to the moment, to focus, to be here now.

Movement catches my eye and I abruptly look towards it, unsure I've seen correctly. There was no noise, but there on the far left screen I see it.

A man crouched low, crawling slowly, trying to blend in with the place, looking more and more like a gargoyle. I stare at the screen, bewildered. What is he up to? Where is he going?

Roland stands up quickly beside me. We both watch the screen, waiting to see what happens next. Troy seems to be heading for the exit. That means he would have walked right behind us to get down the hall to the stairs. How did we both miss it? We'd been so caught up with fear from the revelation of what having these files in Troy's possession might mean, that he'd been able to stride by completely unnoticed.

Except now we could see him.

His features are mostly obscured by the lack of light, but the white soles of his sneakers were easy to detect in the grainy black and white screen. Every moment he inches closer to the doors I feel my stomach drop lower.

He's escaping.

If I were to poke my head out of the control room, I might even be able to catch a glimpse of him before he disappears entirely into the shadows of the stairwell, then out of the building and gone forever.

Yet, I can't bring myself to leave the makeshift safety of this room. Now that the air has settled around us, it feels rather comfortable here, like a warm blanket. I've gotten used to the pressure and thickness of my breathing and I feel sleepy, like I just want to stop running and lie down. A stress response no doubt, but not one of self-preservation.

Hesitating between letting Troy escape and stopping him, we quickly consider our options. We're still armed with the objects from our search, but we know Troy has the keys to the manor and could easily leave before we can get to him. He might even be waiting for us to confront him in the dark stairwell where we wouldn't be able to spot him in time. He has the advantage of familiarity with this place. Having worked here for a while, he knows every nook and cranny.

Part of me wants to let him go. What's done is done. We might as well wash our hands of this and let the beast go. We might actually make it out of here alive. It goes against all my instincts to run after him now. But just as I'm about to admit this, something stops me.

I have an idea.

"Roland, do you still have your phone on you?" I ask, my words rushing out quickly.

"Yeah, why?" He looks over at me, confused. "It doesn't work," he reminds me, showing me the lack of bars.

"But the camera app works, right?" Taking the device from him, I scroll to find the camera button and snap a picture of the files on the desk—for safe keeping. Things have a way of disappearing around here.

Giving it back to him, I ask, "Can you pull up that picture of the map you took of Salter Square?" His eyes grow wide as he catches up with my train of thought.

We might not know the building like Troy does. We don't know all the corners where he might try to hide from us, or how to avoid the cameras, or where to find the best weapons, but at least we're not going into this completely blind. The map will give us some insight, a direction.

Our heads press together as we lean over Roland's phone, staring and zooming the image to expand the section of the manor in which we find ourselves. Swiping urgently at the screen, we reach the section of the plan where we can locate the exit Troy is headed for. We hold our breath, closing in, getting a bird's eye view of the manor. It feels strange to look at a floorplan of the place you're standing in the middle of.

How ordinary it looks when it's just lines for walls, boxes for rooms, and semi-circles for doors. There's none of the looming dread, the darkness, the eeriness we feel now. The map—pure white—feels safe. The dimensions and separation seem to accentuate all the different spaces which is a stark contrast to the final product of the place, with its dark corners and large furnishings. It's difficult to imagine that it's the same place. It looks so innocent on Roland's phone, not evil like it feels now.

But isn't that the truth? Evil is not an appearance, but a feeling. You can't know how a place feels just by looking at its floorplan. You have to walk through the building to feel the energy of a place to feel the history, the pain, the cold.

Roland's fingers move quickly over the phone's glossy screen. His phone is struggling to keep up as the image slowly comes into focus. When it's finally loaded, we peer at it with urgent interest.

There, under the exit steps, is an entrance to a cellar type of basement which seems to expand across the entirety of the manor. It's difficult to imagine how large it truly is. I picture endless space, echoes bouncing off the walls. Then, why did it seem that the group had been congregated together, packed tightly like sardines?

"There, that's where he's keeping them." Roland points with his index finger, using his short nail to indicate the exact spot he believes the group is being held.

A small utility room. The only space in the basement with a door. A space so tiny in comparison to the immense space of the rest of the basement, I had completely missed it. It was barely a closet.

"That's tiny!" I exclaim, appalled. "They must be on top of each other," I add, my lip twisting, suddenly feeling guilty for thinking about sardines only seconds ago. How accurate my imagination had been to what transpired makes me shudder.

We're still bent over the small screen when a loud boom resounds suddenly from down the hallway, followed by bloodcurdling screams. The piercing shrieks tear right through me, and I almost drop the phone in shock. We stare at each other and begin to race down the hall towards the screams.

CHAPTER 30

My legs feel heavy as I race down the hallway. Roland has already reached the exit door. My breathing is deep as I push through the feelings of nausea. I know I need to go back in that dark stairwell—I have to. There's no other way. All those people—he's done something to them. I just know it.

I use the walls for support as I reach the end of the hallway. My head is spinning making me dizzy. I stumble on the last few steps. The constant intake and output of adrenaline is driving me insane. It reminds me of that time in high school when my friends and I drank back-to-back pots of coffee during a group study session just to ensure we wouldn't fall asleep. We didn't, but we were also left with racing heartbeats, nausea, and jittery and pulsing muscles.

My heart is not made for this type of stress. Everything in my body wants to curl up on the floor, to pull my arms and legs in close, for warmth and protection until I fall asleep, blissfully uncaring of my surroundings.

I wish I could ignore what's happening, but I can't. It's all too real. I'm not asleep. This is really happening—whatever this is—and I'm stuck in the middle of it.

Pushing open the door, I catch a glimpse of Roland. Racing ahead of me, he's already reached the bottom step. I peer over the railing briefly and see him kicking angrily at the basement door below me.

The screams intensify with every passing second. I race down the last few steps and within moments I'm standing right behind Roland.

It doesn't take me long to figure out what's going on. Right below the door to the basement, something is seeping through the tiny crack between the door and the floor.

I see it before I smell it. Smoke.

"Holy shit!! Roland!" I look over to him, my eyes big as saucers. I don't need to say anything. He's already thinking the worst, just like me. Troy has set the manor on fire.

"He's going to burn us all alive!" I scream, panic overwhelming me.

Roland stops kicking the door momentarily to look at me and extends a hand to grab my shoulder.

"Stay with me, Laurel. We're not dead yet. Help me get these guys out of here. I need you." His tone is steady, but his eyes are pleading—wild. He's scared, too. I can see how tired he is, just as I am, but he hasn't given up. The fire extinguisher is useless right now as the fire is on the other side of door. It would be easy to feel hopeless and to give up, but the look in Roland's eyes gives me the strength I need to pull myself together.

I need to transform my fear into anger, to use it to my advantage. That's what's going to keep me alive. That bastard wants to incinerate everyone so that there's no evidence of what he's done, of who he is. I feel sick and cover my mouth. I thought burning people alive was something only found in history books.

My scalp begins to itch uncontrollably and I scratch it roughly, feeling immediate relief. It seems that the glue from the electrodes is reacting to my sweat, the wetness triggering the glue to begin releasing its hold on my head. I shake the thought away, I need to focus.

The stairwell is empty. Troy must have been here to set the fire as some point, but he's long gone now. Did he escape through the exit door? I push on the door handle, but it doesn't budge. We're still locked in. He must have locked it behind him when he escaped.

I stand next to Roland and pound the door with my foot as hard as I can following his example, but I end up hurting myself with the first kick.

"Damn it!" I yell, limping backwards. I crash into the wall, the pain shooting through my leg. I must have sprained my ankle or something.

Roland turns back to me, concerned, but I wave him off quickly. He needs to keep trying to break through that door. The smoke is coming out in thick clouds now. *How much time do we have?* I wonder. Although the building is built solidly, I seriously doubt it can withstand a fire.

Refusing to feel sorry for myself, I stand up and ask Roland for his cell phone. He hands it to me, but it's clear he doesn't understand what use it would be to me as there's still no signal. Resolute, I begin to climb up the stairs as quickly as possible. I have a plan.

But when I reach the top of the stairs, I hesitate. Can I really do this? My ankle is throbbing. I can feel my shoe getting tighter as it begins to swell.

I'll have to push through it, to ignore the pain. There are people depending on me. I hear Roland yelling behind me, but I keep pushing on.

Limping down the hall, I make my way towards Room Five where Madeline Cloutier, a mother of two, spent her last moments. She was completely isolated despite being surrounded by others while she was tortured and killed by a very disturbed man.

The brutality of how Troy left Madeline is hard to take. The blood has stopped flowing and is beginning to clot. It now reminds me of ketchup smearing the tops of diner tables. I believe that if I touched it, the blood would be sticky—but I don't dare touch it. No good could come from that. This poor woman has been through enough already. Madeline doesn't need her body to be disturbed and prodded by any more strangers. She deserves respect. And that's why I'm here, despite my gut protesting and threatening to spew food everywhere.

I force myself to look at her and remember every detail of her face. The scene is so ghastly, so eerily fitting with its surroundings. Postmortem, Madeline's facial muscles have relaxed and her face rests slack. I could easily pretend she is part of the manor, a lifelike gargoyle perhaps, but I cannot. I will not. She was a real person, a mother, a woman who deserved better than to be taken at the hands of a monster. Yes, I'm scared and it's unbelievably difficult for me to look, but I know I need to. If we're all about to burn, I want Madeline's life to be remembered. Even for a few moments.

My life doesn't matter in comparison. I'm just a student. I haven't done anything special with my life. I'm sure Xavier and my family would miss me, but Xavier would likely get over it before the year is over and move on.

No one depends on me. No one's life revolves around mine. I might be missed, but my death wouldn't be earth shattering.

The thought surprises me and stirs up a realization that I hadn't considered. I might die at any moment. This old wood paneling makes the perfect kindling. The whole place is like a matchbox. We have no way of knowing how quickly the fire will consume the building. Has Troy lit the entire basement on fire, or only the utility room? If the flames started in the basement, how long before they reach the next floors?

Remembering an elementary school fire safety drill, I crouch and place my palm flat on the floor. It's warm. The fire is growing. We're running out of time.

CHAPTER 31

Lifting Roland's phone, I fiddle with it until I find the camera button and inhale a sharp breath. Inching slightly closer, I take a picture of Madeline's body. I move around her and snap several more from different angles. If this crime scene gets torched, and by some miracle we find a way out of here alive, then I hope I'll be able to get these pictures into the hands of the right people.

They're big ifs, but I have to try. I feel responsible for this woman's death. Troy had been after *me*, but Madeline paid the price. Her entire family will blame me for her death. My throat feels dry, and the pain returns in my ankle.

Time to keep moving.

Limping out of the room, I make sure to close the door firmly behind me. I remember that firefighters recommend closing your bedroom door at night to help keep fire and smoke out as much as possible. I've seen pictures of blackened, burnt homes, but where a door had been shut, there was minimal damage to the inside of the room. I hope that by closing the door, it will help preserve the crime scene.

Madeline's family deserves to get answers. As awful and traumatizing as it is when someone dies, we always want to know how and why.

Back in the hallway, my head low, I jam the phone in my pajama pocket for safekeeping. My index finger scrapes against the broken toothbrush, nicking the skin.

I'd forgotten all about it already. I bring my hand up to suck on the blood, but then remember that I haven't washed my hands since looking through everyone's belongings. Thinking better of it, I use the sleeve of my sweater to wipe off the trickle of blood. Lifting my sweater sleeve, I note that the shoelace is still securely in place on my wrist.

It seems silly now, our hunt for weapons. What good is a broken toothbrush and a shoelace against a roaring fire? If anything, having these items has given us—hope. That's worth it, I guess. But if it comes down to it, I doubt it will save our lives.

I begin to make my way back towards the exit to find Roland when I stop short. The hallway has fallen silent.

There is no longer the resounding pounding of Roland's kicks or the loud screams coming from beyond the stairwell. I refuse to dwell on what this means. Closing my eyes momentarily, I inhale, willing myself to calm down. I swallow, but my throat is like sandpaper. It's painful, but more so is the realization that all those people have most likely been burned alive. I have to hold back the nausea. I feel it burning in my throat, threatening to come up.

To think that I'm next makes my knees weak. Of all the ways I ever imagined I'd die, this wasn't it.

The smell of smoke is getting worse. It clings to my hair and my clothes. I cover my mouth to protect my lungs, but it seems futile. The fire is growing stronger. Looking down the hallway, I try and think quickly of a plan. The bathroom.

I make it to the bathroom in a few painful steps. I need water for my throat. I have no idea where Roland is, if he's still trying to pry the hinges open with the Swiss Army knife, or if he's been taken over by the smoke. I must hurry.

Once I'm at the sink, I swing open the lower cupboard doors and crouch to look for something I can use. Other than toilet paper, there's nothing there. Standing up slowly, feeling the soreness of my body, I see the hand towel hanging from a towel bar fixed to the wall positioned slightly above the countertop. I yank it off the holder and shove it into the sink, turning on the water at full capacity. Once the towel is drenched, I squeeze some of the excess droplets into my mouth and swallow, ignoring how unsanitary it is.

My throat burns—I need this.

Placing the towel over my head, my shirt slowly gets soaked by the water running down my neck. I don't care. I run to the men's room and repeat the steps with the hand towel there, except this time, I don't swallow any water, saving it for Roland. Assuming he's still conscious, that is.

Feeling a prick of panic in my chest, I hurriedly exit the small space and stumble out into the hallway once again.

A flash of green to my left catches my eye. For a brief moment, it almost looked otherworldly—ghost-like—as though it was flying just above the ground by a few inches. I can't make sense of it until I see a second identical shape moving in unison next to the first one. After a beat, I realize I'm staring at pant legs. Someone is running through the grand hall.

Troy.

My hand absentmindedly finds the broken toothbrush in my pants' pocket and I grip around it over the fabric, reassuring myself that it's still there.

Without giving it another thought, I begin creeping towards him. Thoughts of fear and internal alerts go off in my brain, urging me to run the other way, towards safety, towards Roland. My fear seems to amplify in my head, making it throb with its own heartbeat, but I quickly push the thoughts away. I can't stop here. To turn away now would be admitting defeat. I'm probably going to die in this place, but I still have a choice: die fighting, or wait for death to engulf me in flames.

With every step, I feel my ankle's protest. My body is begging me to stop, throwing in random back and shoulder pain for good measure. Anything to slow me down and divert me from my plan. My throat begins to throb, my feet hurt, and I'm sweating. Fear has come. Yet, I know—I just know—that this is something I must do. Not for anyone else, but for me. I can't let the fear win. I can't let evil win.

Troy can't be the last person I see before I die. He can't be the last memory I have. What he's done—what he's doing right now—is despicable. He's getting away with it all. Why does he get to win? Why does he get to have his way? It makes no sense. Cutting corners, lying, cheating, and killing. Since when is that the path of winners?

Am I making a mistake? I stop short and try to catch my breath. What am I going to do when I catch up to him? Can I really take on this guy? I shudder when I remember what he's capable of. When I remember the knife, knowing without a doubt that, given the opportunity, Troy won't hesitate to use on me.

Don't go there, I plead with myself. *Don't think like that.*

Closing my eyes, I prepare myself as images come regardless of my warning. I can't push them away.

Fine.

Let the memories flow through me. Let me face them head on and not cower away. I need to understand. I need to stop pushing everything away and letting them consume me. The intensifying smoke makes me recall a time from my past that I'd forgotten. The memories of a night years ago float around me in swirls like the smoke, bringing me back to that moment long ago.

The night air makes us feel alive. We're sitting on a sandy beach, a roaring bonfire in the middle. There are many of us lying around on the ground, surrounding the fire, trying to stay warm. I'm clutching a pink cooler, condensation dripping onto my hand as I wave it around, animatedly, speaking enthusiastically, feeling the freedom of the night before me. Wearing white shorts and thong sandals. I've got my legs stretched out on the sand, and I feel on top of the world. I'm free, happy and having a good time.

My hair is fashioned in two French braids, my silly attempt to tame my waves. I'm sure many strands have escaped and are floating around by now, making the tight braids look frizzy. It's not at all the look I was hoping for, but nevertheless, my hair is still contained, pulled back from my face, for the time being anyway.

I've got way too much make-up on. I've spent an obscene amount of time getting ready for tonight, taking extra care to sweep my eyelids with the perfect cat line of dark eyeliner; I've put on glittery pink shadow, and taken great care to contour my face with bronzer. I wear a new coral blush on my cheeks, but I can feel them growing hot as the night grows colder.

My tank top is so tight, I have to work hard to remember to suck in my tummy all night. It's getting harder to keep my stomach flat with all the booze. A friend invites me to dance, and I go along with it hoping it will help to keep me warm, to work through the alcohol, diluting it and blurring the edges of the night, making me more confident than I feel.

A girl from our grade has brought a few joints to the party for us to try. She's brought everything in a metal container. There are little baggies of green herbs and zig-zag papers.

She's meticulously measuring and dividing the leaves into equal parts with a credit card and carefully rolling each joint with the accuracy of a heart surgeon; making them fresh, just for tonight. It makes me feel special—privileged.

I love watching the process. I find myself mesmerized by her ability to be so concentrated, so precise, when it's pretty evident that she's already quite buzzed. It's my first time smoking a joint. It makes my tongue feel fuzzy. Passing it around in a circle, I hear myself giggling as we each take turns sucking on the end, inhaling, and holding it in a moment too long as though we're old pros at this.

After a coughing fit, the burn of the smoke enters my lungs and clouds of white smoke exit through my nose. At first, I don't feel any different. The anticipation and the daring feeling of doing something I shouldn't be doing is what hits first. The high comes next. I'm surprised at how quickly it comes on. It hasn't taken long before it messes up my perceptions—in a good way. I love how it makes me feel dizzy, as though I'm floating on a cloud. It's a feeling like no other. Like I'm invincible—untouchable. Even for just a moment.

Without a care in the world, I sit on the sand and watch people dance, closing my eyes and feeling the music pulsing through my body. Swaying in place, I feel free.

As the night goes on, I smoke another joint and drink a few more coolers. That was a mistake. I shouldn't have mixed booze and weed. Especially not when I'm not used to it.

The beach is bustling with people, girls in short summer skirts, lifted so high you can see the half crescent of their butt cheeks. They are sporting tight bikini tops instead of shirts, even though it's dark out and no one is planning to go swimming—well, not yet at least. The smell of stale cigarettes, cheap beer, and weed cling to our bodies.

The outline of a guy—a cousin's friend—is illuminated by the glow of the flames as he approaches me. His mouth is in a sideways grin. He's older. I'm shocked that he's noticed me. He's looking right at me, coming closer. He pulls me up from the ground, takes my hand, and guides me to a darker part of the beach where the tents are set up.

The walk there is blurry. I'm more out of it than I'd thought. I should probably return to the fire, but I stumble forward trusting the grip holding my hand, holding me steady.

The glow of the fire is dimmed. I hear the sharp sound of a zipper being closed and recognize the thin fabric of a tent allowing a faint amount of light through from the faraway fire. I feel cold, craving warmth. I want to tell him, this guy, but I can't find the words. My tongue feels thick in my mouth. It doesn't move right.

For the first time, I realize that I'm in trouble. There's no one else around, no one to come to my rescue. I've willingly gone with this stranger away from my friends, away from the light, and I've allowed him to lure me into this dark, secluded space. I'm too high and too drunk to fight him off. My vision is unfocused, but I see the glint of a sharp knife. I'm so terrified that I freeze.

I allow his hands to touch me as they please while his hungry eyes devour my body. I feel sick. His mouth is wet and smells foul. His tongue jabs in and out of my mouth, making me want to gag. He isn't gentle. I'm a means to an end. I don't even think he's enjoying this. His movements are rough and desperate. He's simply fulfilling a need. I could be any girl. This has nothing to do with me specifically, other than I'd been easily drawn away from my group of friends. Had I not agreed to follow him, he would have moved on to someone else.

I close my eyes and wait until it ends. Once he's through, I push past him clumsily, hearing him panting alone in the tent as I quickly pull my clothes back on as best as I can. Stumbling to rejoin the rest of the party and the rest of my friends, somehow, I manage to put all my clothes on properly, no tags out. No obvious signs of my mistake.

Spotting my friend chatting with a boy by the fire, I beeline towards her. I comb my fingers through my hair doing my best to straighten up and act normal. Refusing to let the tears fall from my eyes, I force myself to keep it together deciding that if I pretend I'm fine, then I'll eventually feel like I am.

Once I reach them, I slump down onto the sand. Oblivious to my sudden disappearance, she offers me a Jell-O shot from a nearby cooler. The rubbery, cherry-red mixture has been infused with so much vodka, I inadvertently scoot away from the fire afraid the tiny glass jar might shatter and explode right in the palm of my hand.

Tilting my head back and closing my eyes, I bring the glass jar to my lips. The overly sweet artificially-flavored gelatin slides down my throat and I force myself not to choke on it. Despite how disgusting it tastes, I do like everyone else and poke my tongue inside the jar to sweep at any remnants of the Jell-O.

Around the fire are dozens of hazy faces, some I recognize, and others I don't. Word of the party has gotten out and people from nearby schools have joined in.

Try as I may, I find myself unable to recognize the guy who took me into his secluded tent. All the faces have begun to blur together. I choose not to dwell on it and simply declare this a crazy night. A guy, a girl, booze, weed, and sex. That's what parties were all about, right? No big deal. Next time, I'll be more careful. I won't mix alcohol and drugs together ever again. I enjoyed feeling relaxed, but not out of control.

Snapping back to my current surroundings and thinking back to the drawing Roland found in my sketchbook earlier, I know now, without a doubt, that the guy at the party had been Troy.

I never knew his name back then, otherwise I might have recognized it and made the connection. It had been a dark night, with limited lighting from the fire. The perfect cover. A way to get away with anything and come out scot-free.

My inebriated state at the time might have been the reason I hadn't been able to sketch him with much detail. Maybe my inability to remember him, compounded with the necessity to forget that unfortunate night, had caused me to not be able to muster many details. It hadn't been a dream, but a terrible night. A real-life nightmare.

It's so clear to me now. I'd almost managed to push it from my memory, but the smell of the burning manor has brought it all rushing back, assaulting my senses and almost knocking me off my feet. It feels so real, almost as though I'm there again in the tent, unable to speak, feeling the sand between my toes, tasting the sweetness of the cooler and the Jell-O shot, smelling the weed and fire clinging to my hair. Unfortunately, you can't convey smells in a sketch. If that was possible, I wonder how many other memories I'd be able to dredge up.

I guess some things get seared in our brains forever, no matter how much time goes by, or how hard we will them to disappear.

CHAPTER 32

No longer caring about my sprained ankle, I lurch forward and run as fast as I can towards where I last saw Troy. I know the truth now. Unlike last time, I'm not sleeping, and my senses have not been influenced by anything other than an overwhelming need for revenge and anger. I'm ready to face him.

Even without a sprained ankle, sprinting is definitely not my strong suit. By the time I reach the main entrance of Salter Square, I'm panting and stop to catch my breath, my hands on my knees. The wet towels are cradling my neck, soaking my clothes. Strands of hair dangle down the sides of my face, my messy bun coming loose and bobbing on the top of my head like a broken bird's nest. I rip the elastic out, pulling several hairs out along with it. Snapping it onto my wrist next to the shoelace, barely feeling the sting of it.

Breathing through clenched teeth, I reach the grand hall entrance. My stockinged feet slide on the dark marble floors and I almost fall in my haste. In the large fireplace, angry red embers glow faintly. No one has bothered to add more logs to the fire throughout the night. The sweat under my armpits has turned cold, leaving me chilled. I vaguely wonder what time it is, but it hardly matters now. The fire in the basement will consume this whole place quickly enough. I wonder if marble burns. You would think that a place built as solidly as this would somewhat survive the flames, but then again, what building stands any chance against fire?

I slow down my pace as I'm beginning to look like an ice skater on this slippery floor. My eyes dart around furiously as I attempt to see anything that might be out of place in the dark. It takes several seconds for my eyes to adjust and for the shapes and shadows to become easier to discern. However, even with my improved vision, I still see no sign of Troy anywhere.

Of course, he knows this place very well. He's got the advantage. His desire to keep his secret is strong and empowering. It serves him well. He's gotten rid of almost anyone who could divulge his secret. Except Roland and me, that is.

A sinking feeling overwhelms me. Unless he's already gotten to Roland. Where the hell is Roland anyway?

Feeling alone and saddened by the thought that Roland might be dead, I feel myself giving up. Doubt creeps in and I begin to second-guess my actions. How can I possibly do this on my own? I just want to go home. I want this nightmare to be over.

Part of me would love to put this all away in a deep, forgotten cabinet in my mind, lock away the file for good and throw away the key. Having Roland by my side had given me strength and made me see parts of myself I never knew were there. But with him gone, his absence leaves a void inside of me that is quickly being filled by fear. And the worst part is that I am allowing the fear to consume me.

How will I confront my demons on my own? I have no idea. I'm not ready for this.

The light from the kitchen pantry is still on, like a lighthouse in a storm. It gives me direction and helps to orient me, helping me create a mental map of the darkened space all around me.

I wonder for a brief moment if Troy has hidden in the kitchen. There he would have access to knives, lighters, heavy pots and pans and who knows what else. It seems like an obvious choice to me now. How did we miss it earlier? We could have looted the place, armed ourselves with usable weapons.

I say a silent prayer that Troy didn't have time to hide in there. I hope he noticed that I was coming after him and I hope I scared the shit out of him. Even if I don't feel strong, maybe my presence alone is enough to scare him, my very existence a threat to his freedom.

Scaring is an art after all. Anyone can learn how to do it, even a small, petite girl like me. Think about how many horror movies and books feature small girls or even dolls. There's something terrifying about defying logic. How could a tiny, fragile girl cause any harm? Then when they do, it shocks us and makes us fear everything. It makes us doubt everything we ever knew.

Maybe it will be enough just to fake it. Remembering everything I've ever learned or seen that is scary, I can use it to my advantage. Knowledge is power.

I think back to late-night reality television shows where grown men would enter old homes out in the middle of nowhere and go down to the basement with night vision cameras to search for evil spirits. Viewers craved the adrenaline rush of being scared out of their wits. Why do you think most horror movies get released around Valentine's Day? There's something alluring and exciting about fear. Movie companies have been making money off of our fear for years. So, what is it about being afraid that works so well? Why do we keep coming back?

Thinking back to the late-night shows, it's obvious to me now that it was all staged to draw you in and to scare you. The slow pace as they walked down the creaky steps to the chilling basement. The dark lighting coming from a single lightbulb hanging from the ceiling. Even the way people talked in agitated, urgent whispers, forcing your ears to pay extra attention, leaning in your seat to hear better. Then came the brisk movements they would make when they thought they heard something behind them, the sudden flickering of lights, a loud noise in the dark corner, the description of feeling of a cold breeze in their hair.

Everything was fair game. They used all the senses. And I could use them as well now to my advantage, all without being any kind of monster. Because when it comes down to it, it's child's play, a game of distractions, setting the stage, creating the opportunity for heightened emotions and tapping into someone's fears.

I don't know much about Troy, but I know he's scared right now.

Not of the dark, or of how creepy this place is. But scared to go back to jail. So scared of being caught and exposed, that he's deviated from his usual pattern and has burned and killed people.

He is locked inside this manor with Roland and me until he knows for certain that all evidence of his crimes has been destroyed. I know he plans to kill us, but I'm not sure how. There's no doubt in my mind that he's capable of it either. He won't hesitate when he gets the opportunity.

His fear is strong. He's been leaving trails behind, making mistakes. He's desperate. Good. I can use that.

Momentarily distracted, I slip on the glossy marble and fall hard on my knees, palms outstretched to soften my fall. Carefully standing up, crouching slightly, I see my reflection in the dark floor. The embers illuminate it ever so slightly, creating a mirror-like image. My hair is a mess, a curly mane around my head, and my eyes are wild and intense. I step back, shocked.

I look exactly like the mystery woman from my sketch. I am her. She was in me this entire time.

Maybe I just needed to come to terms with what Troy had done to me, what had happened back then. It was enough fuel to make her come alive in me. Surprising myself, I realize I'm not afraid anymore. It took all of this to bring back the memories of what really happened at that beach party. I had blocked it out, refused to allow my mind to go there, but now I know.

Now, I'm ready to fight. I've got nothing to lose.

CHAPTER 33

Gathering myself, I stand up taller than I ever remember doing before. A sly smile plays on my lips. Finally, the confidence I needed this entire night is coursing through me. I don't need anyone else—not even Roland. His absence hadn't caused me to become hollow. I'd felt empty because I hadn't believed in myself. I didn't think I'd had what it took to confront Troy on my own. But I know now that I am strong. I have it within me. It's been in me this entire time. Troy will not win.

I'm about to check the kitchen when I spot a shadow crawling up the stairs. The circular stairwell has the perfect hiding spots, so I'll have to be careful.

Ignoring my aching ankle, I begin to climb the stairs two at a time. When I can no longer see the grand hall, I slow down my pace slightly. I have no idea what's waiting for me up there. Troy has the advantage of being up higher and having a better view of things. For all I know, he's been watching me slip-sliding across the floor, destroying any credibility I might have thought I'd gained in the last few seconds. He must be laughing at my pathetic attempt at redemption. Like David and Goliath, what's so scary about me? At least David had a sling shot. I only have half a toothbrush and a shoelace.

Before I begin to doubt myself, I shake the thoughts off. *No.* I almost scold myself out loud. *I can do this.*

I need to see this through. I need to fight for the younger version of me. I owe her this.

This time, I've got my wits about me. I'm not drunk or high. I'm mad and motivated. I want to hurt him with every fiber of my being, but I know I need to keep my head clear. Being fueled by revenge will only cloud my judgement. Hadn't I just told Roland something similar? I'd even stopped him in his tracks, scared he might put himself in danger. No. That won't be me. I need to think. I need to be smart here. There's no room for mistakes.

Fighting the insecurities around doing this on my own, I search within me for that strength I've only just found again. The girl I sketched wouldn't let people walk all over her. She wouldn't cower and wait for death. She'd fight for her life. She'd stand up for herself and for what's right and she wouldn't allow her boyfriend to treat her like crap. How did I get so far from that?

I want to be more like the girl I sketched.

Scratch that. I *am* like that. It's always been inside me. But the fear of being disliked, of being judged or being left alone has smothered that part of me like water on a hot fire. There was a time when I'd had this spark, a confidence and strength deep within me pushing me forward, but somewhere along the way, I'd lost the heat. Just like Roland's sister, I'd lost my spark. Troy had drenched it with water and attempted to put it out completely. For years, he'd succeeded. But right now, here, in this moment, I feel that fire burning inside of my belly. I know that's exactly who I need to be.

Creeping up the steps slowly this time, I decide on another approach. Troy already knows I'm here. How can I use that to my advantage? He knows I'm coming, but he doesn't know how fast. My speed is one of my only available variables.

He'll assume I'll be standing, walking up the stairs, like any normal person would do. He wouldn't naturally be expecting me to crouch, crawling up the stairs one by one slowly, like an animal, putting me directly in line with his knees.

One advantage I have at my disposal is that I know the anatomy of the body. As someone who spends hours sketching portraits of others, I've learned a thing or two about how the body works—how it bends, how it folds on itself, where there is more fat or bone.

From the way Troy was running earlier, I could see that something was wrong with his right knee. Maybe Sadie fought him and he fell down the stairs earlier, or this unexpected running around had caused an old injury to flare up. The thought that Troy might be as out of shape as I am makes me laugh momentarily.

Whatever it is, however he got hurt in the first place, it's just the kind of edge I need to beat him.

Carefully, I pull out the broken toothbrush from my pocket. It's been practically impossible to forget its presence since my finger scraped it earlier and it's been poking my thigh since. I examine it again closely. The handle is plastic and hard—solid. The break isn't clean. Sharp prongs stick out, making it the perfect weapon to plunge deep into Troy's injured knee, forcing him to slow down, hopefully doubling over in pain, and inevitably weakening him to become an easier target. I don't have it all planned out yet, but I don't need to.

This will work. It has to.

Crouching low like a feral cat, I slink up the stone steps on all fours in my best attempt to be stealthy. This is an area of the manor I haven't explored yet, and I'm rapidly starting to doubt this approach.

What if this has all been a trap? Troy will have lured me into this dark space away from everyone just like he's done before. I realize now that this must be his signature move—isolating his victims, catching them off guard.

It's not remarkably brilliant; more standard and expected. How did I fall for it, again? I'm so annoyed with myself that when I reach the top of the landing, I almost miss Troy who is crouched in a gargoyle-like position, watching me silently.

I barely have time to register the glinting reflection of a sharp blade as it cuts through the dark, aimed in my direction. At the last moment, I lift my hands to protect my face. The blade punctures my skin, cutting through it like butter. The knife pierces through my left hand for a split second and I watch it slip out as Troy pulls back, winding up, ready to use it again.

The pain of the wound comes seconds later, as the shock wears off. I yell out in agony. My scream resonates back to me, bouncing off the walls, making it sound distorted and growl-like. It's not a sound I remember ever emitting in the past and I hope never to hear it coming out of my mouth again.

Whimpering, I don't dare look at my hand. There is no sense in being quiet anymore. He's already found me.

Standing up quickly, I rush to a corner of the hallway and hurriedly wrap one of the towels hanging from my neck around my injured hand. The pain rushes through my entire body and I see stars behind my eyelids. I struggle not to pass out. I can't believe he stabbed me, but he did. Now my blood stains the floor of this place, seeping into the cracks, where it will remain forever.

This is real.

I'm losing a lot of blood, but I don't think it's enough to be life threatening. I can't tell if I've lost all function of my fingers. There's simply not enough time. I consider wrapping the shoelace around the towel to secure it in place but decide against it. Every second counts. Instead, I just clamp my other hand around it to hold it still. It will have to do for now. At least until I can get far enough away to tend to it properly.

A growl shakes me back to the present moment just as Troy lunges at me once again, making me fear for my life. I take a deep breath, realizing I've forgotten to breathe and bite my cheek to keep from screaming again. There is no blood tricking inside of my mouth this time. Maybe I'm running out of it. The thought is frightening, but in a strange way, it gives me courage.

I won't make it easy on him. If he's going to kill me, then I will fight. I want him to suffer.

Leaning hard against the hallway wall facing the stairs and hugging my hand to my chest, I don't feel up to the challenge. I feel every ache, every sore muscle, and my head feels like it's splitting in half. My whole body feels heavy, my eyes want to close, and my ankle throbs, refusing to let me forget its presence. I want to sink to the floor and cry.

My mind races a mile a minute, retracing my steps, looking for holes in my strategy. Trying to understand where it all went wrong. How did Troy know I was coming upstairs crouched like that? Was it his quick reflexes that had made him hurt me first? Had I been too slow?

As Troy advances towards me quickly, I spot something I hadn't seen before. In the corner of the ceiling, aimed halfway down the stairs and down this corridor is one of those convex security mirrors placed to warn people of any other person coming up the stairs. Elsewhere, the marbled stairs would easily announce someone's presence, their footsteps echoing against the hard surface, but here, the carpeted upper floor would muffle the noise.

That must be why the mirror had been placed up here and not down on the main level. It was the first one of its kind I'd seen in this place and it looked strangely out of place with the rest of the architecture. I'd missed it because I'd been crouched, so intent on getting to Troy first. Had I lifted my gaze by a few inches, I'd have seen it. Troy had used it. He'd watched me coming and known exactly where I'd be.

Frustrated and hurt, I feel myself losing hope.

Troy strides towards me, slowly. A menacing smile splayed across his face. He thinks he has me cornered. I try my best to ignore him. Watching that mirror, I mentally curse it, but also feel a surge of anticipation. In it, I see Roland cautiously making his way up the stairs, sneaking around. My position acts as the perfect distraction. Troy's back is turned to the threat approaching him from behind.

It's the perfect plan.

It's as though we had planned it this way. It was our advantage from the beginning. Two against one. So simple, we almost missed it. Roland had repeated it so many times—together. He'd insisted on it. Why had I gone off on my own to take pictures? I should have waited for him. It had been a mistake.

And then, of course, I'd spotted Troy and had wanted to fight him on my own. But for what purpose? To claim the victory on my own? Out of pride? To seek revenge for the past? Because I had something to prove? It was probably the latter.

The night terror had exposed a part of me I never knew existed. There was a fighter in there, itching to come out. Hadn't I hurt Xavier that night? I wonder if there was an underlying reason I instinctively wanted to hurt Xavier. I wasn't conscious during my night terrors and I couldn't remember what we'd been doing, but maybe my subconscious had been working on overdrive, awaking to protect me even in the oblivion of deep sleep and fighting for me when I couldn't. This inner strength I was quickly discovering had been within me my entire life.

My parents had named me Laurel, which stands for victory. It's time to honour that name. Just because I don't do it alone, doesn't mean I'm not strong, or a winner. This is about so much more than winning. This is a fight against everything that has held me back. It's about putting right a wrong. It's about finally defeating evil.

CHAPTER 34

Roland eyes me with intensity, communicating without using any words. His cheeks are streaked with black soot giving him a warrior-like visage, as though he's intentionally prepared for this very moment, gearing up with war-paint to offer him courage. From the looks of it, it's working. He's ready for a fight.

He lifts a finger to his lips, urging me not to give away his position. My role in this plan is to act as bait and keep distracting Troy. It's me he wants after all. I need to keep his attention on me.

My mind does summersaults trying to understand the timeline of all of this. Troy must have gotten to me only days or weeks after attacking Reese. His desire must have spiked after assaulting her. He must have found me in that strange reprieve between attacking her and getting caught, counting on one last joyride before she'd had a chance to come forth with her testimony.

I feel sick to my stomach, but I can't let it show. I stand my ground, pushing myself against the wall, trusting its construction to hold me up. Roland's presence and reassuring gaze give me confidence. I feel safe with him. My heart flutters fleetingly. Could I be having real feelings for a man I've only just met?

If I listen to my head, I would say it's most likely because of the situation we're in, and that the moment it's over, and the shock settles in, I'll realize how arrogant I was to assume I felt anything but grateful for his support and help during this ordeal.

Maybe Troy is the glue binding us together, a sick shared experience. His sister and I, we've lived through similar things. Maybe that's all it is, a certain affinity.

But it's more than that, deeper than that, isn't it? If I listen to my heart, I know it definitely is. I'd felt the pull towards him even before knowing all of this. I know he feels it too.

It's in the way he looked at me a little too long and the way his hand lingered near mine. I felt it radiating off his body when we were standing next to each other. We're connected.

Part of me doesn't want to break this connection we have, this invisible string linking us together. If we succeed against Troy and get out of this god-forsaken hell hole, what will happen to us, to this thing we've begun? Will we simply go our own ways, back to our lives never to see each other again? For some reason, I can't bear that thought. It's too painful.

We're a team. Since he pulled me to safety, we've been a team. He needs me now. We need to do this, even if it breaks the spell we're under. I bite my lip, doubtful. I don't want this to end, but I do want Troy to be stopped. More than anything.

The smoke is thick around us. It acts as a buffer, but it also makes it difficult to breathe. My throat feels hoarse again. When will this end? Sweat is dripping down my forehead making my head itch once more. The fire is stronger now. We're running out of time.

Like a shark in the ocean, hunting for injured, bleeding prey, Troy has his eyes on me. He wants to finish the job. He wants what he didn't get the last time. His desires have escalated since the first time we met.

It's no longer about sexual gratification. It's about humiliation, about power over another person, about holding the life of another in his hands, and being the almighty one, the one to decide another's fate. His eyes are black—pure evil.

He's so fixated on his desire to hurt me that he makes a terrible mistake. He assumes I am alone. He's stopped paying attention to his surroundings. It's a crucial mistake.

Roland jumps on Troy's back, making Troy stumble, off balance. He drops the knife, leaving it to fall with a soft thud on the ground. It's not at all threatening now; it's the very opposite of how it felt only seconds ago when Troy had brandished it up high, about to use it on me.

While the men are wrestling, I lunge for the knife, narrowly missing being kicked in the side of the head by Troy. Roland's got him from behind, holding on tightly to his neck. Letting go of my own wounded hand, I reach out and grip tightly onto the knife's handle. It's slippery from sweat and I almost drop it. It's heavier than I thought it would be. I can't picture myself using it, but I will if I need to. If Roland starts to lose his hold on Troy, then I'll have to swoop in and save him.

Troy's eyes bulge as he glares at me holding the knife. My right hand is intact, thankfully. I raise it up and the blade shines against the full moon peeking through the windowpane behind me. The rain sounds even louder up here on the second floor. The steel roof accentuates the sound of the heavy rainfall. The storm is right above us. What I wouldn't give to pull back the roof and drench the fire, extinguishing it completely. It's getting harder and harder to see in here.

I approach carefully, but without holding the towel with my right hand, holding it in place, the towel around my left falls to the ground exposing my wounded hand. Roland looks up for a second, worry etched all over his face. I see him release his grip on Troy ever so slightly, and I realize with horror what's going to happen. Troy has been waiting for such an opportunity, for Roland to become distracted, and takes advantage of his inattention.

I watch in dismay as Troy uses his body weight to throw Roland over his shoulders, over the railing, but at the last second, Roland grips tightly onto Troy's scrubs. The room is silent as both of them curve over the edge of the balcony and plummet to the floor below.

My mouth gapes open. No words come out. No scream. Not even the roaring fire makes a sound. The time seems to slow down. I feel my feet move forward, my good hand reaching out into the empty space where they'd been standing. But they're already over the edge, free falling to their deaths, and there's nothing I can do.

CHAPTER 35

$\mathbf{A}$ sickening crack resounds through the manor as they collide with the floor below. The force of their falling bodies has fractured the marble floor. Several tiles have large, new cracks spreading through them which expands as the men struggle to their feet.

Miraculously, they are both still alive.

Mesmerized, it takes me a beat before I scamper down the steps brushing my right hand against the wall for support, my left hand still hurting too much to grab the handrail.

By the time I get to the bottom of the stairs, Troy has lurched to his feet, leaning slightly to the right, blood dripping down his forehead, barely keeping his eyes open. When he sees me, a disgusting smile crosses his lips. His mouth is full of deep red blood and he appears to be missing some teeth. With dread, I can see that he's not through with me yet. Eyeing my bloody hand with a twinkle of excitement shining in his eyes, it's clear that he's enjoying my suffering. He's standing between Roland and me, blocking my way. I feel trapped. He's closer to me than Roland is to him. I watch him consider his next move. He's not stupid. He knows he only has one shot at this.

I chance a quick glance towards Roland.

He's leaning against a large, marbled column that I hadn't noticed before, but it's impossible to ignore now. My heart aches as I see him gripping his shoulder tightly, wincing in pain. He seems to be holding up his arm. He must have dislocated it, or broken it.

There's a pool of blood on the ground that smeared as the men fought on the floor. Tracks in different directions indicate that they've had time for a few swings at each other before I made it down the steps.

I'd lost sight of them for only seconds while racing down the circular stairs, but the descent had felt like an eternity. Not knowing what I would find once I reached the bottom had been awful. Who would still be alive and who would be dead?

The blood is a dark circle—thick—implying a deep wound for one of them. Or maybe it's just how blood looks against black marble. I see a bloody handprint on the wall near Roland and deduce that he's the one bleeding. He needs helps. We need to find a way out of here. Urgently.

We're all injured, circling each other like vultures, in a standoff position waiting for someone to make a move. I could kick myself for leaving the knife upstairs. In my haste to get down here, I'd left it behind. I hadn't expected either one of them to still be alive. That had been foolish of me. I know that now. We're not safe until Troy is dead and we manage to get out of here.

In a flash, I see Roland's eyes switch from fear to fury.

In my moment of distraction, Troy has limped towards me as quickly as he can. Roland can't react fast enough to trip him or slow him down. I stand there paralyzed. My options are limited. Instinctively, I step back until my back hits something sharp.

My good hand reaches behind me and I grab a fire poker conveniently stored on a rack beside the fireplace. Without even thinking, I swing it in front of me intending to hit Troy over the head but at the last moment, I jab it forward as hard as I can just as he slips in the pool of blood on the glossy floor.

246

The poker stabs him, piercing through his chest with force, impaling him right in the center of it while emitting a disgusting wet sound. I feel the weight of his entire body on the end of the stick. I realize that I'm holding him up and I drop my arm, letting the metal stick fall and clatter to the ground. The weight of his body falling drives the poker in even farther, piercing through his back.

Splatters of his blood cover my entire body, leaving me shaking from the shock of what I've just done. My arms are speckled with dark splotches, like when I was in kindergarten splattering white paint with a toothbrush to appear like snow. I lick a speck of it off my lip. I shudder at the metallic taste of it, desperate for a glass of water to wash it away.

He'd been so close to reaching me.

Roland comes up next to me now and places a hesitant hand over my shoulder. His attempt to comfort me goes practically unnoticed as my eyes glaze over, my body becoming numb trying to protect itself.

The sight of Troy is ghastly, but I don't scream. I just stand there— completely immobilized. Roland is speaking, but I don't hear him. Everything has gone mute—as though every sound is being filtered through a thick pane of glass. Roland's voice is distant like I'm underwater. I watch his lips move and see the urgency in his face, but I can't move. I barely react to his touch.

I did this. I killed Troy. Oh my God. I've just killed someone. I'm going to jail.

A mixture of emotions filter through me all at once. I know I'm in shock, but I'm also incredibly relieved. But that feeling is short-lived—guilt and disgust quickly take over. I fear for my future, while also feeling victorious at having defeated evil.

We've won!

I start laughing hysterically. I'm a mess.

I must look deranged. I barely recognize myself. It's as though I've been broken apart and someone has put me back together, but the pieces don't fit quite right. That's what's become of me. It's confusing, messed-up, and horrifying all at once.

I feel a tug at my hand and realize Roland is pulling me urgently towards the door.

"We need to get out of here!" I hear the desperation in his voice.

"But how?" I bellow, utterly baffled.

We're screaming over the roar of the fire which is getting louder the closer it gets to us. The flames are all around us now. With a sad realization, it's clear to me that after all we've been through, we won't make it. With every other exit blocked off by the overpowering flames, there's only the main entrance remaining. Yet, without a key, it's doubtful that we'll have any chance of opening the door. If it's built like the rest of this place, all that's left for us to do is to wait for the flames to devour us, keeping our souls prisoners forever. I guess I can't expect a better outcome. I did just commit a horrible crime after all, even if it was in self-defense.

I don't see any way out of this.

We have only minutes before we die of smoke inhalation and before our bodies are consumed. It's hard to focus when death is imminent, but at the same time, my mind goes into overdrive. *Survive*, it seems to be saying from some deep desire inside of me.

The flames are most likely visible from the outside of the building now. They have reached the roof, waving in the early morning like a beacon, summoning help without any of us having to call. I'm sure someone will have smelled the stench of burning and seen the smoke. Even in the dark, it's thick and overwhelming—you can't miss it.

If we're lucky, fire trucks might already be on their way to rescue us. We might be saved in time, but we can't afford to wait for that chance. We can't just sit around and do nothing. We have to try to save ourselves first.

Removing Roland's phone from my pocket, I begin walking towards the nearest window. Balling my hand into a tight fist, careful to place my thumb over my fingers to keep it from breaking, I punch my right hand as hard as I can in the middle of the window, but it doesn't budge.

"Damn it!" I scream out in pain, cradling my hand. Both hands are hurt now and I feel defeated. "I wanted to throw your phone out there for someone to find," I begin to explain through tears. "I took pictures as evidence. People need to know what Troy did here. How he killed everyone. Especially that woman—her family deserves the truth. Everything will disappear in a few minutes. They'll never know the truth!" I wail.

Watching me, Roland takes my hand and gently coaxes me to hand the phone over. I reluctantly give it back to him, my hope completely diminished. He grips it tightly and motions for me to wait there. I wouldn't be able to move even if I wanted to.

The flames can't come fast enough. I just want it to end, for them to take me away now. I want it to be over already, but this night keeps dragging on, keeps teasing me, making me hope and then taking it away.

Through the smoke, I spot Roland hovering over Troy's body, and for a sick moment, I think he's about to take pictures of what I've done to him, as though it's not burned into my head forever as is this entire night.

I can't close my eyes without seeing the revolting images of tonight's events. They play over and over like a projector set on a loop. It wouldn't be the worst thing to never have to think about this ever again. The greatest regret I have is that I never got to tell my mom that she was right about Xavier and that I'm sorry for not trusting her judgement. I'll never get to make amends with her and fix what I broke.

What kind of a life is it to reach the end and only have regrets? I thought that when my time came, I would have been in a place to feel grateful for the time I'd had, the opportunities I was able to experience, and the people I'd met. But when it comes down to it, my life has been nothing more than a big lie, an embarrassment, a gaping hole that someone else will fill without much trouble.

Roland has leaned over and is patting around Troy's pants. *What the hell?* I'm appalled until I realize what he's doing. Triumphant, he beams as he lifts up a lanyard with keys on it. Throwing the keys over his neck, his one hand holding the phone and the other rendered useless due to his earlier fall from the balcony, I watch him struggle to move Troy's body.

What is he doing now? I ask myself.

Ignoring his request to stay in my spot, I begin to move towards him.

With one good arm, Roland is pulling on Troy's leg, inching him closer to the fireplace. With a sick realization, I understand. He's going to torch him like he did to the others. And eye for an eye so to speak. Reserving judgement, I can see this is something he simply must do for his sister. He doesn't know yet but he's also doing it for me. In a way, getting rid of the evidence might be beneficial to me too.

I decide to help him. Together, and with great effort, we heave Troy's heavy body into the remnants of the fire. Quickly, the horrible smell of burnt flesh enters my nostrils. I want to gag, but we can't stop now.

We hurry to push the rest of Troy's body inside the large, cavernous mouth of the fireplace and, leaving him behind to burn, rush to the front door as fast as we can. I've got second-degree burns on my forearms and on my back and so does Roland. I can see the wounds on his arms and wish I could take his pain away.

The keys burn the tips of his fingers as Roland struggles with his one good hand to sift through them trying to locate the one for the front door. He tries one but the keys slip from his grasp. We can barely hear them clang on the floor. Loud banging against the door makes us back up instinctively, just in time. Mesmerized, we watch as the large door swings open, letting in a delicious gust of fresh, night air. The cold burst of air sears my skin and I cry out in pain stumbling to the side.

Several firefighters rush inside and scan the room quickly, directing us urgently, and escorting us outside towards safety.

CHAPTER 36

Several emergency vehicles wait just outside the doors. Ambulances are parked sideways on the lawn, their flashing lights blinding us.

Stepping through puddles without a care, I realize how far I've come and the price I had to pay to get here. I'll never be the same again. Gritting my teeth, I feel the rain sting my burnt skin, but the pain feels good. It reminds me that I'm alive.

We're guided to the closest ambulance and immediately paramedics get to work. They place us directly on stretchers, strap us in gently, carefully avoiding our burnt skin, and without any delay, they begin treating us for smoke inhalation. Intravenous liquids from a clear bag hanging on a hook in the back of the vehicle starts to flow into me and it isn't until then that I allow myself to feel everything I'd been holding in.

My body starts to shake beyond my control, and a blanket is carefully draped over my shoulders to help with the shock. Next, they fasten oxygen masks to our faces before we have a chance to say anything. In between their quick movements, they tell us the police are on their way to record our statements.

The manor is surrounded by curious and concerned neighbours who've been woken up in the middle of the night by the loud sirens racing through their quiet street or by the cloud of smoke rising in the air coating their houses in its passing.

"Is there anyone else in there?" A firefighter asks me, urgency evident in his readiness to leave my side and rush back into the burning building. I look over to Roland before shaking my head solemnly. He looks down and his shoulders slump.

"There's a small utility room in the basement," Roland says after removing his oxygen mask. "There are many people piled in there. Troy Robinson locked them in before he torched the place," he adds gravely. He places the mask back over his mouth indicating that he's done talking for now.

Solemnly, the firefighter nods, a grim expression on his face, and his shoulders slump. Even though they managed to save two of us, this night will probably still be seen as a failure. Too many lives were lost, even if they were taken before the fire started. It's obvious that they take this blow personally. I want to reach out and tell them they couldn't have changed the outcome, but I need to keep my mask on. My throat feels like needles are piercing through it, making even swallowing a great effort.

My eyes meet the firefighter's for a brief moment and we seem to understand each other. We had both wanted to save the others, but neither of us had been quick enough. I watch his back as he quickly turns towards the building, quickly being engulfed in angry flames.

I spot Liz, the receptionist, amongst the curious gawkers in the crowd. She looks much more normal in her flannel pajamas and fluffy rabbit slippers with her hair down, almost like someone I could hang out with—almost. She catches my eye, then turns around and quickly walks away to fiddle with her phone. She's no doubt calling the building manager.

Roland had given his phone to an officer a few moments ago. They will begin an investigation into Troy and determine the identities of all the people who died tonight in order to contact their families. We are taken to the hospital which happens to be right around the corner from the clinic and are triaged fairly swiftly. I guess having a police escort helps to speed things along.

"You guys are lucky. Neither of you will require any skin grafting," the doctor announces cheerfully after checking out our worst burns.

A small victory for us then.

"You got out right in time though. Some of these will take a little over three weeks to heal, but they should be fine with time," she adds encouragingly.

Part of me hopes that I won't scar so as not to carry around a constant reminder, but another part of me knows that scar or no scar, I'll never forget this night, no matter how hard I try. Some scars are on the surface, but most aren't visible. You can't ignore them, even if you can't see them. They are persistent and always present. Those are the hardest ones to heal.

What Troy did to Roland's sister will stay with her forever. Reese has suffered and been marked in a permanent way. Troy's actions will have a residual effect on each and every interaction she ever has with anyone ever again. He made sure of it. There will forever be an unmistakable hint of doubt and fear clouding everything she does, blocking any light that might try to seep through.

I still have to tell Roland what Troy did to me. I've decided that sharing my story with him might indirectly help Reese recover.

Facing my own fears and speaking up about it might help her to know that what happened to her isn't due to anything she did wrong or could have done differently. Troy was just a bad man who took what he wanted, no matter the consequences or the wreckage he left in his path. He destroyed things, hence the smoldering building.

Who knows how many other lives were ruined by this man?

I feel my stomach turn as I realize that in the next few moments or hours, unsuspecting families will wake up to find police at their door and will hear the worst news of their lives. I just wish we could have saved them. I heard one policewoman mention that she'd seen the hinges on the door had been pried open, slashed at with a small blade. While they were trying to work out who had opened the door, I already knew.

Roland was looking down at his hand, his one arm fastened in a sling to keep it secure until he saw a doctor and had x-rays taken. He'd worked so hard to break open those hinges and it had finally worked. The door had opened, but he'd been too late. He will most likely feel guilty about that for the rest of his life. I tilt my head in his direction, willing him to face me. He needs to know that he has nothing to be ashamed of. He did the right thing. He tried to save them—risked his life trying to save them. We had very little at our disposal.

I still can't believe we missed the fire poker set until the very end. It saved our lives. We'd gotten sidetracked by the control room and hadn't ventured further into the building while scavenging for weapons. I push the memory of Troy's distorted face away from my mind.

The police have asked us to describe him, and I mentioned that I could attempt to draw him when my hand gets better, but there's hardly any use now that he's dead. If anything, replicating the drawing might help other survivors come forward and heal parts of their pasts.

Unrecoverable, my precious sketch book was destroyed in the fire, of course, along with my other belongings and everyone else's.

Surprisingly, I don't care at all. I've realized that there are more important things in this world.

It takes several hours for the fire crew to get the flames under control. Thankfully, there were no other buildings in the near vicinity which allowed them time to focus solely on crowd control and reducing the damage.

As the building wasn't deemed a heritage building, despite the persistent efforts of the community, the city's reluctance to award it historic status had paid off. The firefighters only had to worry about saving living beings, not hundreds of precious gargoyles and irreplaceable antiques.

A sleep clinic should be a place to rest, to get answers, and hopefully to heal. But this place would now always be remembered as a torture house, a place where the sick ruled. Where many died the night it burned to the ground. It will mark this city forever—a sore spot—a blemish.

As it turns out, the marble fireplace remains somewhat intact after the fire, a little more porous perhaps, but still standing. Almost everything else had been incinerated, including the remnants of Troy and all his victims tonight.

I think of the businessman's little girl in a pink onesie, or the married man with a wife at home sleeping peacefully not knowing what's happened. It's too horrible to dwell on, but I do it anyway, out of respect. To remember who they were rather than how they died.

That's what's really important here.

Not how Troy ended their lives. Not as victims, but rather as heroes. People who fought for their lives and, in death, helped to bring to light the crimes of a horrible man, stopping him from hurting anyone else ever again. If Troy were still alive today, he'd wish he were dead. Part of me wishes I hadn't granted him that favour.

CHAPTER 37

A few weeks later

I lift my leg and prop a thick, fluffy pillow beneath it. Nova fluffs another one to place behind my back so that I can lean against the wall. My right hand is wrapped tightly in an itchy, white cast that I've been decorating as best I can with my rapidly healing left hand. Ambidexterity is proving to be a challenge, but I'm determined to keep trying.

My right ankle is still swollen but recovering nicely. The dark purple bruises have faded to a sickly yellow which, strangely enough, means that I'm healing normally. Under the advisement of my family doctor, I've got an appointment with a well-known nutritionist to evaluate my diet and eating habits with the goal of improving my sleep and strengthening my bones. She's also unofficially prescribed regular exercise as a stress release.

My burns have blistered, and some have already popped. The process has been excruciating, but then so is being burned alive. I've held my tongue, clenching my teeth through the pain. I refuse to complain about my predicament. I'm home, I'm warm, and I'm safe.

"I have to confess something," Nova says as she moves from behind my head to face me. "I'm in way too deep with this and I need your help to keep me accountable," she sighs. "I debated even telling you, but then your accident happened, and there just never seemed like a good time..." she rambles on.

That's what people have been calling it—almost getting murdered and burnt alive—an accident. Which, I guess, is accurate if reduced to its simplest form. But living through something like that seems like it should be called something much more epic than an accident. A feat, a trial, something like that. Survival.

"What's going on, Nova? Look, you can't possibly shock me after what I've been through," I reassure her, tilting my head in her direction as I wait patiently for her to speak. She twists her hands together, struggling to formulate the words. The anticipation is killing me, but I stay silent. *I should probably start using a different expression*, I think grimly. *Something less dramatic.*

"Well, I kind of started a business on the side," she starts. I nod encouragingly. So far, I'm failing to see what the issue is.

"Okay," I probe her. "What kind of business?"

"Well, see that's the thing. It's not entirely legal..." She looks away at that.

"Will you just spit it out already?" She's driving me crazy.

"I posted an ad online to rent out the spare room for an hourly fee to high school kids." She waits a beat seemingly gauging my reaction, but I don't follow.

She continues, her words running together as she speaks quickly. "You know, a place where they can go, away from their parents, to...well," she blushes, "you know..." Wincing at me now as I start to catch on, she squeezes her eyes shut.

Even to herself it sounds ridiculous.

"Nova! Oh my God! You did what?" I'm astonished. Despite seriously doubting she could surprise me, she's done it.

That explains all the strange people, her so-called 'friends,' who kept coming around and the noises coming from the spare room.

"I know! I know, it's awful! I'm a horrible person! I feel so bad about it," she admits, wringing her hands like she's trying to squeeze guilt out from them. She slumps on my bed heavily, deflated. "What am I going to do?" she asks me seriously.

"I can't believe you did that! You had me thinking I was losing my mind." This explained so much. "Some of them stole things, you know." I point out.

"Yeah, I know. Ashley told me some of her stuff went missing the other night." She sighs heavily. "Look, I know it has to end, like, right away. It wasn't cool of me to put everyone at risk like that. Letting strange people in our house, even if they're young, it wasn't right."

"It was pretty fucking stupid, actually."

A tiny smile plays on her lips as she looks up coyly. "But I did manage to make quite the profit."

"Nova!"

"I know, I'm sorry! Well, let me at least make it up to you." she pleads. "I'll get you a new sketch pad, one with the thick pages you love and some new charcoal pencils, okay?" I smile at her. I can't help it. She feels so bad. Plus, she said she's not going to do it anymore.

"Okay, fine! But seriously, we need to rent that room to a proper roommate to help reduce our rent. That's the more legit way to go about it, in case you forgot," I point out obnoxiously.

She laughs and stands up. "I know, I know," she agrees with me.

We make a plan to clear out the room and put up an ad for a permanent roommate this week—together.

"Oh, by the way, here's your new cellphone. It just got delivered in the mail." She hands me the square box and I open it.

The phone is so slim in my hand, the screen so glossy. For a moment it reminds me a little too much of the marble floors at Salter Square, but I swallow and the memory is gone just like that. I'm able to compartmentalize things, at least for the moment.

Turning on the phone, I wonder briefly if the night terrors will return any time soon. So far, they've stayed at bay. And that's how I plan to keep them, even though there's practically nothing I can do about it. I like to think that my mystery woman got her revenge the night of the fire. That I got justice for her and in return, she set me free.

Activating the phone takes only a few moments, and I'm suddenly reconnected to the online world, linked to the internet, instantly flooded with texts containing well wishes from worried friends and family members.

Tee has sent me so many messages, urging me to call her back. She and Brian had finally decided to go out on a proper date, and true to our regular pattern, I'd somehow managed to disrupt their intimate moment. On the way home from the restaurant, the radio had announced the breaking news of the Salter Square fire and Tee had remembered me mentioning going there for a sleep study. They'd immediately turned the car around and, regrettably, postponed their date again. They have their make-up date planned for this evening and I've promised to remain in my room and out of trouble.

My mom is coming over tonight to take care of me and I'm ready to apologize to her, finally. We have a lot of talking to do and I've learned quite a bit about myself since the accident. Not everyone gets a second chance, so I'm determined to use mine. Life is so unpredictable. I don't want to put this off any longer. It's time to own up to my mistakes, but most important of all, it's time to thank her for everything she's done for me; for always having my best interests at heart, and for loving me no matter what.

Scanning through the list of lit up names, I begin feeling overwhelmed. It will take me ages to respond to all of these. Sighing loudly, I place the phone down on my nightstand and resolve to only answer a few at a time and pace myself.

There's one number that I won't be transferring to this new phone—Xavier's.

He came rushing to my house after hearing from my parents about the fire. Since my phone had been destroyed in the fire and I'd been in the hospital, he'd been trying to reach me for several days when he found out what had happened. He'd driven through the night to knock on my door and see me. The moment he stepped inside my room, he got down on one knee and proposed.

It seemed that he'd done some thinking during our time apart and my 'accident' had been the wake-up call he'd needed to appreciate what he had with me.

It came as a complete shock.

It wasn't easy, but I'd learned a lot about myself at Salter Square. There was a lot about myself I didn't yet know, but one thing was for certain.

I did not love Xavier anymore, nor did I still think he was a good match for me. He got angry and fought me for a while, said I'd wasted two years of his life, and that he could do better. It was hurtful, but in the end, I know I'd made the right choice.

I couldn't go on living a lie. It wasn't right.

What I'd gone through had changed me. For better or for worse, I'm stronger than I ever gave myself credit for. I deserve to be happy and to be with someone who both respects and adores me, for me. I don't want to have to survive another tragedy for him to appreciate my value. I know what I have to offer, and my next partner should see it also. From the start.

Roland's text comes through with a soft beep, and I smile, reaching for the phone. I send him a quick reply planning on a video chat later on. Holding the device feels normal. It feels like I'm on the right path, like I'm taking control of my life again.

Only this time, I know how strong I truly am. Now I know that I don't need to run away from the dark shadows or the ugly parts of my past. All of my experiences make up who I am. They are a part of me, and I must embrace them or get hollowed out by them.

I've seen ugly. I've torn it apart, dissected it to pieces. It didn't frighten me any longer. It has lost its power over me.

I'd had this strength within me the entire time.

Now I know with confidence that if I ever come across another monster like Troy, I'll be the one chasing and he'll be running for his life.

ACKNOWLEDGMENTS

This story was so much fun to write, and I hope you enjoyed it! Although it is completely fictional, I know that sleep disorders affect many people in different ways. After hours of research on sleep, electrodes, brain waves, stages of sleep, dreams, and night terrors, I did my best to stay as true as possible to the facts, but nonetheless, if mistakes in accuracy were made, they were entirely my own doing.

I owe many thanks to my husband, John, whose personal experience as a participant in a sleep study helped to spark my interest in creating a story by using this setting. With inspiration from repeatedly watching the animated movie, *Beauty and the Beast,* with my daughter over weeks being in lockdown during Covid-19, I used the famous castle as a benchmark to describe the architecture and grandeur of Salter Square, hence the mention of the famous circular staircase.

I'm incredibly grateful for the insight and devotion I received from my beta readers, Krista Walsh, André and Danielle Landry, Heather Budd, Natalie Banks, and John Young, who kept me grounded and true to the genre.

A very special thank you to my editor, Sherry Torchinsky, for your insight and exceptional skills, and to Laurie Holbrook for providing a quote for the cover.

Thank you to the readers and friends who have motivated and encouraged me to write and who read my words. Without you, these stories would remain locked inside my laptop or gathering dust on my bookshelf. I'm glad they have found their way to you. More and more, I realize the importance of storytelling and my role in it. It's a wonderful privilege as well as an incredible responsibility.

I hope reading my story offers you the escape and joy it brought me to write it. Enjoy!

ABOUT THE AUTHOR

Michelle Young is the author of *There She Lies*, *Your Move*, *Salt & Light,* and *Without Fear*. She holds an Honours BA with a major in psychology and a minor in communications from the University of Ottawa. Young lives in Ottawa, Canada with her family.

If you enjoyed this book, please make sure to leave a review and follow Michelle Young on Facebook, Instagram and Goodreads.

Facebook.com/michelleyoungauthor

Instagram @michelleyoungauthor

www.michelleyoungauthor.com